Streets

of

Melted

Gold

An Arguably Fictional Memoir

Brittany Maylyn Du Bois

To my parents –

Don't worry; I'll be OK.

To my sisters –

Don't worry; we'll be OK.

To this island –

Don't worry; it'll be OK.

*"You will never say goodbye to the past,
until you understand why the flashbacks haunt you."*

— *Shannon L. Alder*

Acknowledgments

I'd like to acknowledge my parents for being the best character models a girl could ask for. Thank you, Mom, for your random island knowledge. Thank you, Dad, for all the quotations that lingered long enough for me to write down. My two sisters - Nicholette and Suelyn - thank you, for sharing my experience. Thank you, Mrs. Supplee, for that push to dig deeper than my mind allowed me to go. I'll never forget my experience with the Carver Center literary arts class of 2016, and my best friends Sriniti and Zosia for personally tolerating my nuttiness. A second thank you goes out to Zosia once again for the gorgeous cover art. A thank you goes out to Conor, who became very special to me over the past couple years. And thank you, Ronnie, my beautiful cousin whom I laid my eyes on for maybe twenty minutes total, for letting me borrow your name while you're away in Heaven. I am grateful for those who have somehow, whether they know it or not, ended up in this novel. Without you, without my learned ability to observe and wonder, there would be no story. Thank you for a great story.

Author's Note

I know exactly what you're wondering: what the heck is an arguably fictional memoir? Well, that's what this is (surprise). It is a memoir because the narrator is recounting and reflecting upon a sensitive time in her life. It is fictional because the narrator is not me. It is arguable because the narrator could be me, or anyone else who was born across the border or across the sea. The narrator could be you.

And if it is not you, then pretend it is you. That's the point. The United States is no longer a stranger to immigration, but it still acts as though it is. The beginning of this story takes place in a country with no name. I assure you, it's a real country, and I make no effort to hide this fact – I'd just rather you not associate the story with a specific place. I believe the story is much bigger than the country of origin. I've heard many immigrant experiences growing up. They seemed to all be extreme, heartbreaking, and unsettling, and it's a shame not everyone can hear the cries of these people. Now what if it were you crying? What if it were you crying, and you couldn't completely figure out why? What if you were a child with a troubled family, but you can't figure out what exactly the source of the trouble is? Be ignorant. Be knowledgeable. Be confused. Be nosy. It changes you.

It changes me.

Part One

Old Country

House Fire

Our house was your average house. It was single floored with two bedrooms and an outdoor shower and toilet. Early in the morning, the sun hit the outside walls and highlighted every blemish. The sky looked like God personally dropped by and painted a canvas with soft shades of peach and ripe papaya. The air smelled of ocean salt. Our three chickens clucked happily in their coop. I was in the garden helping my mum pluck tomatoes when Dad called me into the kitchen. He asked me to buy a new shovel.

For what?

"For your crap, crapaud." He handed me two tens.

I tossed my damp sweat-rag onto the stove and left.

Meggie's Garden had all kinds of gardening equipment, although no one ever actually used the tools the way they were intended. Just the other day Mr. Jimmy mentioned how he had been using his vegetable pot as a food bowl for his six mutts. I bought a black shovel with a thick green handle and began walking back home across Cuanta Lane's dimpled sidewalk. Mum said to never buy shovels with light color at the bottom because it was never fun seeing your own gifts on a white backdrop. That always made me laugh. Still does.

"Aye, Ronnelle!"

I turned around. Mrs. Sadd was packing a suitcase into her husband's minivan. Her lips were shaped into a squiggly line and I knew she was going to say something smart.

"Your arms broken, gyal?"

I looked down at the shovel which had been dragging across the ground and collecting dirt. Last thing I needed was for Dad to think I bought the shovel used. I held it over my shoulder like a knapsack on a runaway.

"You real doltish, child," Mrs. Sadd hooted with a laugh. Something fell out of her suitcase and I ran to pick it up. The shovel fell by her foot. "Careful."

When I bent to pick up the fallen smock, I traced the patterns of daisies and roses. There wasn't a married woman here who didn't own a house dress with floral patterns.

Where you goin', Mrs. Sadd?

"Your father didn't tell you? I headin' straight for those streets of gold with Mr. Sadd," she replied, folding the dress neatly on the floor of the van. "Streets of gold, I can finally see. Goodbye small world, hello big country."

I never heard that song before.

I picked up the shovel from the ground, hitting it against my calf to get rid of the dirt.

"It's not a real song." Mrs. Sadd laughed and began walking back to her yard. "Go take that shovel home before your parents cut your tail for lapsing."

I nodded quickly and began my run home. The song lingered in my head. I liked it.

Streets of gold, I can finally see. Good bye small world, hello big country.

I forgot the rhythm she sang it with, but I didn't forget the lyrics. They didn't even rhyme and I remembered them. It wasn't the first time I heard the streets of gold talk. It was a silly thing adults had been talking about for the last year, ever since Margaret Jaya, a lady who used to run a roti stand down the street, discovered them and never came back home. My parents hadn't talked about the streets of gold to me yet, but I didn't mind. Golden streets are in Heaven and nowhere else.

I got home, and Mum and Dad didn't show any care about the smear of dirt on the new shovel. They didn't care about the song I was singing to myself either. I met them both in the garden, Mum holding a basket with only two tomatoes inside. I tried to sing the song louder for them but they were walking to the backdoor. Dad flinched when his fingers touched the glass. I jumped.

What's wrong, Dad?

Mum placed her hand on Dad's shoulder while she slid the door open with the other. We all stepped inside, Mum with her tomatoes and me with the shovel. A wall of heat hit our faces.

Why is it so hot in here?

No one answered me. Instead they scrambled towards the kitchen. I ran to them. Did Mum leave the oven on? I poked my head in the doorway and immediately felt even warmer. For the second I was there, I saw flashes of red. Dad scooped me into his arms and ran for the back door again, Mum close behind him. We all flew out of the house. My hands searched for the shovel.

"Ronnelle, forget the shovel and go with your mother."

But Daddy what about the chick-

My collar was grabbed by Mum's bony hand and I found myself being dragged across the garden. We were making a wide circle around the house to get to the front. At the same time, like a scene from a movie, Mum and I turned towards our home. It looked crooked. The roof was caving in towards the middle. I wondered if the chickens were smart enough to try to escape. The window – the one that my cousins and I had always sat under when we did our homework with sunlight to keep the power bill low – shattered. Nothing touched it. It just shattered.

"Sean!"

Smoke poured out of the house into the sky, tainting it with grey. Dad came running to us, his head whipping back over his shoulder again and again to look at our home. His overalls were streaked with a black dust. I reached to touch it but he smacked my hand away.

"The fire started in the kitchen," he said, looking between Mum and me.

I stared at him. His wide eyes settled on Mum.

"Kim, you were boiling rice? What happened?"

"I'm not sure, honey-"

It was my fault. I knew it. I left the rag on the stove before I left. It was me.

"The papers were in the house, Kim! The papers!"

15

It was me, but I didn't say anything

Mum placed her hand on my shoulder as if she knew it was me. "I'm sorry, Sean. I don't know what happened."

From our safe distance, I sang the song quietly to myself as the attention turned from me to our average house with one floor, two bedrooms, the papers Dad seemed to love more than our shovel, and a rag left on the gas stove. At the same time, my father and my house exploded. I didn't know which one was easier to look at.

Streets of gold, I can finally see. Goodbye small world...

I forgot the rest.

The Step-House

Dad called it the *step-house*. He said it's the evil version of our old house. It was still single-floor and two-bedroom, but now Mum, Dad, and I shared a room, and every night I woke to the sound of the mutt chained to the pipe outside. His name was Butch, a middle-aged Retriever-mix, and he was technically ours now that we lived here, but he was having trouble realizing it. By here, I mean Grandma's house. Dad's mum. Or, Dad's step-mum. I didn't call her Step-Grandma because that took too much work and Mum said it wasn't worth the trouble with her. I didn't know what that really meant, but I figured she was supporting my decision.

Grandma slept in the room next to ours. It was a small room, but bigger than the one she let us borrow. At least that's what Dad told me. I wasn't allowed to go inside of it for any reason. And, "under no circumstance" was Mum or Dad allowed either. Especially Mum.

Our room had two beds smashed against each other to form one big one that took up half of the floor space. It was fun for the first week – the bed was spacious and Dad said funny things when his eyes were closed. Now it was tiresome. Mum got a cold and snored so loud she woke up Butch on the other side of the wall. He barked and then *I* woke up and both Butch and I found ourselves listening to the sound of Mum's throat congestion. Sometimes I stuck my head out the window above the smaller bed and watched Butch's ears twitch to the beat of the snores. When he caught me, I shut the window quick and laid back in bed.

I wanted to see inside Grandma's room. I wanted to know if she had enough space to pull open her dresser drawers. I knew we didn't.

Every once in a while I heard scratchy male voices late into the evening, such as this one. I pushed my ear against the thin walls separating our bedrooms, but Mum, as usual, heard the cry of the bed beneath my movement and gave my bottom a good slap.

"Go to sleep, nah." She hardly moved her mouth when she spoke to me in the darkness.

Instead of pointing out how funny she looked half-asleep, I said okay, though I didn't move. I knew she'd fall asleep again as soon as I stayed still for a bit. Then my ear was back to the wall and I was hearing the voices again. They were deep and rumbly, making the wall shiver when the volume got louder. They pronounced every letter when they spoke, like the 'r' in lover and the 'h' in thrilling. When the voices died away, they were replaced with heavy breathing. Then sleep.

I woke up the next morning to the sound of light laughter and my neck hurting. I had fallen asleep last night with my chin hooked on to a bulge of paint on the wall. Mum and Dad had been looking at me with big smiles. They called my neck a trooper before heading off to work. Dad sold cell phones that flipped. He hoped with the new slimmer model he'd make more money. I told him I didn't think so because no one wants a phone that can slip through their fingers. Mum worked at a nail salon but when people asked what she did, she talked about facials. I didn't get it, but Grandma said I shouldn't bother to figure it out as long as they raked in the money. It was less exciting when you know how the money got there. I wondered about how Grandma made money, and how she got enough of it to get a TV for her room. Grandpa was up where the *real* streets of gold are, so my first guess was he left her his money.

We never had a television before, but I had seen it through Mr. Jimmy's living room window. That was when we lived in our old house. After school I'd follow his two daughters to their house and stand by the window to watch one episode of Muppet Babies. They didn't know I did that, and they never will, because now we were in the step-house and I had switched to a different primary school. I had watched the girls long enough to know how to set the antennae and kick the TV when the screen faded into itty black and white moving dots. If I could just get in Grandma's room, I could slip in an episode at least once a week while she takes her afternoon nap on the porch.

When the sky was dusted with stars and my parents came home and Grandma hid herself in her room, I was able to leave her door open a crack thanks to the stack of Dad's business cards I left at the edge of the doorway during supper to prop it. Grandma never looked down, so I knew it would work. I was on my knees, squinting my eye through the little space the cards let me see through. I saw a white plastic chair, the kind you put on your back porch but never clean. Grandma became visible when she planted herself in the seat. She was staring forward at something, and I felt myself get excited. It must be a TV. She was in the way, but now I knew she had one. Then I heard Butch barking and a sharp clicking noise. Grandma rose to her feet and stepped aside, and a man was dangling from the window. He dropped himself onto the floor like a professional, and even bowed. Then he grabbed her by her house dress and they disappeared from my vision, and there was that sound of a mattress creaking against two bodies.

"Did you hear something, sweetheart?" Grandma. The word *sweetheart* sounded so alien coming from her. Unnatural.

"No."

I heard that similar deep voice with the pointy accent. The pitch changed between high and low – he seemed to have his own different voices. Here the voice was clear, but I still felt that familiar rumble against my skin with each shake. If I remembered correctly, heavy breathing should begin... Now.

My eye stared at the empty space that Grandma had been looking towards moments ago, alone in her chair. From that moment on I vowed to never peek into Grandma's room ever again. There was no TV. Just an open window.

A Word in the Neighborhood

My new school wasn't so different from the old one. I still had to wear a white button-up, a blue skirt way past fingertip length, and high white or blue knee socks. My shoes looked like the infant version of flats – the ones you find in the shoe department that were originally flats, but to keep on the baby's foot, they add a strap and buckle. They clicked against the floor and it made me feel like a teacher. Or my mum when she slipped out of the house early in the morning for work. Whatever it was, I sure felt important.

In front of the building, Mum nudged me on the head before walking across the street. My new friends Marissa and Tamika were standing behind me, single file, just like Mrs. Seepersad liked it. Just like any school teacher liked it. I wanted to turn back and say good morning to them, but Mrs. Seepersad was already standing by the door, hand up. All the girls in my line and all the boys in the other line to our left bowed their heads and closed their eyes. I did the same. Mrs. Seepersad recited the Lord's Prayer and we repeated after her. At first she made us parrot every couple words, but eventually, she said, we would say the whole thing without her.

Amen.

We followed her into the hallway towards room 302. I slowed down to get closer to Marissa since Tamika was lost in tabanca for Joel. Her eyes were glued to that boy as if he were a piece of chocolate. Meanwhile, Marissa kept staring at her nails. When she noticed me watching her, she took my hand and looked at my nails too.

She let out a deep breath. "We both gettin' a clout."

I looked at my hand.

"She's checking nails today."

She checked them last Friday.

"She checks them every Friday, Ronnelle."

I began biting the tips of my nails, and Marissa did the same. They were already a little long because last Friday was my first Friday at the school and Mrs. Seepersad had excused me for my nail length. I didn't cut them. At the door of the classroom, I took my last nip. I couldn't spit the piece of nail out –

20

Mrs. Seepersad was standing by her desk with a ruler drawn – so I swallowed it. It poked the inside of my throat. When it was my turn to be inspected, I coughed into my elbow quick before speeding over to my teacher.

Good morning, ma'am.

"Good morning, Ronnelle. Let me see your hand."

My hand was taken from my side into Mrs. Seepersad's grasp. I thought it was going rather well. I managed to bite each nail down the hallway, but the two lines of skin stretching across Mrs. Seepersad's forehead told me my job was sloppy. She rubbed her thumb against my fingernails, the jagged edges scratching against her.

"I appreciate the effort but you have to remember these things." She held the ruler up. "Your body should be clean for the weekend, for Sunday. That means your nails should be tidy and cut."

Smack! On my palm.

I felt my chin vibrate to hold back a sob.

Smack!

It was over. A few of my classmates smirked and giggled as I walked by, but I paid no mind. Just the day before, John got a good whack across his bottom for pulling Tamika's braid, and I had laughed. I settled into my seat in the second row beside the window – my favorite seat. The window allowed me to look at the playground, and just beyond the playground was some bush. The bush on this side of the province was small. It only took twenty minutes to get from one side to the other. Back home, it took an hour. I used to lead my old friends through those jungly woods since they assumed I was the tree expert. I really wasn't – the trees looked the same to me, but I did pay attention to the way they were spaced from one another. The position of where the vines rested on the ground. No one knew the bush like I did.

We reviewed arithmetic and grammar, and during recess I stayed inside to read *'Til the Well Runs Dry*. Mrs. Seepersad adored the book. She said she felt strange about me reading a high level novel, but I told her it was fine.

"What interested you to read books like this?"

My dad is a writer. Read anything and everything.

At lunch time, we were dismissed again to go outside. Tamika and Marissa wanted to go buy doubles from the vendor, so I told them to go ahead; I'll wait on the bench. And I did, with my book and a plastic container of fried plantains on my lap. They were a little dry, the fried plantains, but that was what I got for skipping dinner last night. I wanted to read as much as I could of the book since I had made a bet with Dad that I'd finish it by Sunday.

A few standard two kids darted past me and almost knocked my bowl over. I glared at them, but they were distracted by the football. They kicked it back and forth and my stink eye faded into fascination. Not because it was interesting to watch. You could go to the market and see kids playing football in the parking lot. It was because of what they were saying.

"Leroy told me in America they call this soccer."

"Sucker? Now that's real stupid." The shorter one with the huge lips pouted, making his mouth look even bigger.

"No, soccer, boy! Soccer!"

Soccer?

The boys looked back at me. I hadn't meant to say that out loud.

"Yes, soccer."

That's stupid.

"Yeah, but that's America, ent?"

I nodded as if I knew, but I really knew nothing except that America's streets were possibly lined with gold, and everyone wanted to go there for that very reason. I knew that Mrs. Sadd and her husband were already there, "making it big." And now I knew that over there, they called football *soccer* even though football made much more sense.

The boys went back to their game and I went back to my lunch. I finished my plantains before Tamika and Marissa joined me on the bench. As soon as they arrived, they talked about the Smurfs, and for a while I was interested, especially with the new Smurfette character being added, but when they mentioned Fraggle Rock, I turned back to *the Well*. The girls both had their own televisions and antennas and remote controls at their houses. I figured one day I'd ask one of them if I could come over and watch TV, but not until we got closer. I even considered spending the night if I got lucky. I could wait for them to fall asleep in their beds, head to the living room to play with the channels, and see what I had been missing. Unfortunately, we never got to the sleep-over level.

After school, Marissa boarded a maxi taxi with her mum, so Tamika said she'd walk with me a little before we parted ways at Tampa Road. We collected some water from a standpipe on the way and shared it using a plastic cup she brought from home. She asked me a bunch of questions – so did your last primary school have the same uniform? What does your mum do? Your dad? Did you like your old teachers? How do you like it here? – all questions Marissa had already asked me on my first or second day here. Then she said something about TV and I looked at her. She began to lead the way home.

What?

"I said, do you have a TV?"

I shrugged, but then shook my head. I thought Grandma had one in her room, but I didn't think that was true anymore.

"Why not?"

She seemed surprised. I shrugged again.

"We have one in the den, but Daddy hogs it one hundred percent of the time."

What does he watch?

"The news. But sometimes I climb on his lap and we watch Fraggle Rock."

Again with the Fraggle Rock. I looked down at my shoes clip-clopping against the seesaw sidewalk. In my peripheral I could see the branches of the surrounding trees shivering in the light sea breeze. We got closer to Tampa Road, but I couldn't listen to her go on about her television and antenna and remote control. I walked a little faster.

"Hey! We're going uphill! You're going to give me a Charlie!"

I looked back at her.

23

Mum is waiting for me at the end of the street. I got to run.

"Okay, tell her I say hi!"

I lied again by nodding to her request, and while my calves knotted together like double Dutch rope, I ran up the hill and turned at Tampa. Out of sight, I slowed down my pace and bent over my knees, hands on my thighs. My breath was heavy, sounding like Mr. Jimmy after chasing the same teenagers for stealing things from his roti stand every Saturday. I wondered why I wanted to get away from her.

I thought maybe it was because I didn't want to hear about any more of the things she had that I didn't. It wasn't the TV; I didn't care about that. At the time, I assumed I could come over her house one day and watch whatever I want. The picture that really made me want to run away was the one of her sitting on her dad's lap, the two of them watching television together.

They had time to be happy; I wanted that.

Lenny

Uncle Johnny said he was coming over to drop something off. At least, that was what Mum had told me. I asked her what he'd be giving us, but she wouldn't answer directly. I asked her why, and she shrugged. It made me angry.

"You should feel excited. Fix your face, Ronnie."

My face don't need fixing.

"Don't get doltish. Wash up, he's coming at quarter past five."

I ran to the bathroom to wash off my hands and feet. I had been outside earlier with Grandma's dog, Butch, trying to get him to like me. Mum had a way with dogs, so she quickly managed to get him to not bite her when she approached him. As for me, well, I was standing in front of the cabinet with two bandages strapped side by side on my arm. I scrubbed off the dirt from my palms, and my feet got a scrub, too. I didn't always wash my feet when I walked inside the house – I had done it in our old one, but in the step-house, Mum and Dad didn't scold me for that anymore. As I left the bathroom, Dad sped by with papers in his hand. One floated right out of his grasp and swayed back and forth until it hit the floor. I picked it up. My name was written in bold letters at the top left corner, and then I saw my birthdate, and then the paper was ripped from my hand.

"Did I say you could read that?"

Dad rapped me on the head and disappeared into our bedroom. I thought I said sorry, but I wasn't sure. He wouldn't have heard me anyway. I skipped to the front door to ask Mum about Uncle Johnny again but she wasn't there. The one perk about living in a tiny house is that you can't lose anyone. There was Grandma's room, which none of us were allowed in, the kitchen and living room, which were both completely open to each other, the bathroom, which I had just been in, and then our room. She must be in our room.

I checked the clock on the wall. Big hand on twelve, little hand on five. Just fifteen more minutes. I wanted to go outside again and bother the dog but I didn't want to get sweaty. Instead, I started tidying up. It was a little humid out anyway. I moved my slippers from the front door, and Dad's dress shoes. I stuck a stray plate from the counter into the bottom cupboard where the plastics are. It didn't belong there, but I couldn't reach the China cupboard. Grandma called it that, the China cupboard, because she thought all of her plates were China. Probably still does. Mum would twist her lip every time Grandma said something that wasn't true. She did that every time Grandma called them China. Therefore Grandma definitely didn't have China plates.

The front doorknob suddenly clattered and clinked and I remembered that in the step-house Grandma had that strange rule about keeping the door locked, even when you're home. It was a silly rule, and I thought Uncle Johnny agreed because his first instinct was to just turn the knob, not knock on the door. I opened the door and jumped to hang from his arm. He walked us inside, his arm stretching outward so I could swing freely. Any time I asked about his arm muscle, he said they were so big because of his job. He helped people move from place to place.

"Speaking of moving, I'm here to talk about the surprise."

I yelled for Mum and Dad.

They met us in the living room. Mum gave Uncle Johnny a big sibling hug. Dad did his funny handshake where he smacks his hand against the other person's hand in a variety of ways. Lots of boys did that. I didn't know why. Mum said it was because they're too scared to hug each other.

"I see Ronnie's all ready. Come on outside, Bones."

I ran outside ahead of everyone else. There was nothing new on the lawn besides Uncle Johnny's red pick-up truck. In the back, though, I spotted the top of a wiry cage, and I instantly saw myself holding a fat puppy with big sad eyes and lazy ears. I ran to the truck and tried to jump and grab the ledge of the bed, but I slipped and dropped to my feet again. Then I felt Dad's hand tug me away from the truck. He scolded me, saying something about waiting and how rude it was to touch someone else's "property," but Uncle Johnny brushed ahead of us and slid the cage out from the bed. He stood in front of it. I was having trouble seeing the creature inside, but its fur was long and white with little puddles of brown. I felt myself shaking again. I thought it'd be nice having a friend around the step-house.

Click. Click. The cage opened. There was the sound of feet stepping onto the grass. And a child screaming. I backed up, imagining some sort of devil dog, but Uncle Johnny chuckled and moved out of the way. I found myself staring at not a new puppy, but an old goat.

"This bad-john right here is Lenny, and he's all yours, Ronnie."

I frowned. This wasn't the first time my family got an animal as a gift. We had chickens once upon a time. In fact, we'd had two goats before too, back in the old house, of course. They died way before the fire. What we never had, though, was a puppy dog.

Uncle Johnny tugged on the goat's chain to get him closer to me. He knelt down beside the thing and ruffled his neck fur. The goat bleated. I reached forward to do the same, but the goat jerked back and even prepared to buck forward with his uncut horns.

Yeee! I fell right on my bottom.

Dad and Mum laughed at me. I tried again and the goat stayed still this time. I guessed I had done it wrong the first time. His hard fur pricked my fingers with each stroke, but I kept petting him. He was definitely friendlier than Butch, but that wasn't saying much. I glanced over to the side of the house. Butch was chained up, as usual, but I wondered if bringing a goat into the family would cause problems.

Does Butch like goats?

Mum snickered. "Yeah, if you curry it."

That was Mum-speak for *keep that goat on the other side of the house.*

Uncle Johnny made a big show of looking at his rubber wristwatch. The longest hand wasn't ticking at all, and when I pointed out that his watch wasn't working, he just said something weird: it's a metaphor. It's a *metaphor?* For what?

"I should head out soon. All yuh know how to take care of goats so I don't need to give you his manual."

Where are you going, Uncle Johnny?

27

"Oh, shucks, they didn't tell you?" He looked at my parents. "You tortured my child, ah?"

Dad grinned.

"Alright, Ronnie, let Uncle Johnny tell ya something. Me and Auntie Jemma are heading up. You know what's *up*?"

I tilt my head to the side. Heaven?

"Close. America, baby."

America?

"And this little guy isn't ready for something like America."

America.

"That's right. And it'll be a lot of trouble through Customs if we bring a goat."

All the adults laughed, but Lenny and I stayed quiet. To me, America was just where people on gold streets called football, *soccer*. That was it. Why didn't he think Lenny was ready for it? Lenny was as ready as I was.

After that, Mum, Dad, and Uncle Johnny talked for a bit, but I didn't waste time trying to pay attention to them. I turned back to Lenny and slipped the chain out of Uncle Johnny's hand. Holding the grey metal loops felt good. I felt like I owned the goat. Lenny was my "property." He was mine to keep. We began to walk in circles throughout the front lawn. I giggled at the way his body rippled in each heavy step he took.

Hi, Lenny.

His beady eyes stared forward. He looked like he didn't care about anything – the same look my mum got every time she cleaned a chicken she butchered in the backyard for dinner.

"Lenny's actually a little boy," Uncle Johnny said. "He's just a big little boy. Just like your husband, Kim."

Mum chuckled and Dad pretended to be offended. I looked at my goat.

You're real fat. Did Uncle Johnny feed you lots of sugar?

Lenny stopped walking and turned to look at me. His movements were slow and strong, and suddenly I thought about how he and Butch were evenly matched in size. You can't eat something that's the same size as you, even if you curry it. The two of us headed towards Butch's side of the house. First, I took a peek around the corner. Butch was lying on the grass, his big head burrowing into the patch of dirt in front of him. Even though he had the temper of a goose, he was a cute dog. Sometimes I even felt bad for him. He was real old, and his nose sounded like it was burping while he slept. Yet when his eyes were closed, he was less scary.

So, I pulled on Lenny's chain, and I pulled again, a little harder this time. The chain was a straight line, no slack between us. I pulled one last time and he quietly muttered in goat-tongue and stepped towards me. Then, I guided him over to Butch. We stood less than a meter away from his head. The dry grass crunched beneath my feet and Butch's eyes popped open. I jumped. His dark chocolate eyes zipped between me and the goat, and then they settled on the goat. It's funny – he chose Lenny, a stranger, over me, his house guest, but at the same time, I was happy. If I couldn't be friends with Butch, Lenny could for me. I stepped away and gave them some time.

"Get that pot hound away from my goat!" I heard Uncle Johnny yell.

He was running to me, or maybe Lenny, and Dad and Mum were following after him. I frowned. Lenny was my goat. I had everything under control. Lenny was my "property" and only I could handle him. All of their faces dropped and my frown whisked away because I wanted to laugh and say it's okay, you can't eat something the same-

Thump.

Lenny was on the ground. I was being lifted and backed away from the end of Butch's range. Butch was snapping his jaws and barking at us as Uncle Johnny snatched Lenny away from the murder scene.

The screaming child noise erupted again, but it was a soft vanilla scream. Then it melted through the growling of the mutt and the sound of Dad's hand against my spine. It sounded like Lenny was saying goodbye.

Lenny was my goat for about three and a half minutes. I owned something for three and a half minutes. I wasn't sure what I had been expecting from Lenny and Butch's meet. Maybe I had wanted to see two very different things become friends. Maybe I had thought Butch just needed a companion. Or maybe I had just wanted to see them fight. All I knew was that when Lenny's eyes closed, I felt nothing except a pat on my back.

Screaming Kids

I decided to hold a funeral for Lenny, my formal goat. He died the day before. I hadn't know him very well, but I had known what he was, and what he was was my property. Now he was dead, though it didn't mean he wasn't still mine. Right before bed, I had asked Mum if I could keep him in our room, like a teddy bear.

I never had a teddy bear, Mummy.

"You don't need one. You've got me and Daddy on the bed."

But I shouldn't.

"...go to sleep."

It didn't go very well, and Mum's words were always final. If I couldn't keep my property, I had to bury it, and bury it properly. I invited everyone I could think of – Mum, Dad, Uncle Johnny, Tamika, and Marissa. Everyone except for Grandma. Unfortunately, everyone had plans.

Everyone except for Grandma.

Mum had to go to work. Dad had to go to work. Uncle Johnny was already on a plane, heading "up." Tamika and Marissa's families were out of town to spend their Saturday at the reef. But Grandma was free. She asked me twice that morning about the funeral, not quite requesting an invite, but implying interest. She was paying a lot of attention to me. She even made me breakfast: fried dough smothered in butter and a slice of cheese. While the food had been delicious, my stomach was churning and I couldn't eat more than the edges.

You couldn't blame me – I thought there was a spell on it.

So when she asked about my funeral plans for the third time, I finally put my foot down. I told her she couldn't come. She had nothing to do with Lenny. She wasn't there when Uncle Johnny gave him to me.

"Neither was your friends. What were the names? Paprika and Mary?"

Tamika and Marissa. They're my best friends.

"*Best* friends? This is your second week, child."

At least their dog didn't kill my goat!

31

Grandma fell silent, and I was about to feel good. My statement must have gone through to her – but I was wrong. There was a funny expression on her face, her thin dry lips crooked up toward her eyes. Was she smiling? I tightened my grip on the extra invitation I had drawn up after breakfast. It was just a drawing of Lenny with "x"s where his eyes should be. No information about the time or place. I didn't even have any food planned. The funeral was going to be as modest as his death. As this house. As my life.

"Fine, but let me give you a tip, nah?"

I nodded slowly. Whatever would make her go back to her room.

"When you bury him in the backyard, and you *will* use the backyard – this is my house, don't you forget it – mark the spot above the ground."

As obvious as the tip had seemed, I hadn't thought about it, so I was grateful she told me that. I wasn't sure why she told me. Nevertheless, being able to actually find the spot where my dead goat was buried was something I hadn't considered. Taking her advice and a shovel from the front closet, I went to the backyard. Dad had already wrapped Lenny's body in this black material. It felt like a trash bag. I chose a nice spot in the backyard. It was the far left corner. This way, Butch could see what he had done, but not get any closer. Dogs must feel guilt, right?

As I dug the shovel into the ground, mosquitos began to pick at my arms. I didn't bother smacking them. Anyone who lived near water didn't care about bug bites. I was busy anyways – Lenny's bagged body was beginning to rub me the wrong way and I wanted it out of sight.

It took me a while but I finally dug a hole large enough for a goat. I turned away from the hole to face the funeral audience, or at least where they should have been, and snatched a folded piece of paper from my jean pocket. I smoothened it against my thigh a few times and let out a deep breath. My Lenny was dead, and I had to make this speech the best speech I've ever shared.

Well, I had never written a speech before, or shared one, because I was eight, but this speech was my best one. Is my best one. Right now, that speech is nowhere to be found, and frankly I hardly remember the words. I do remember what I spoke about, though.

For only knowing the goat for maybe five minutes, I found a lot to say. I spoke about how I thought he was a puppy dog at first, because I never had a puppy dog before. I spoke about how I assumed having a goat would be boring, because I had two goats before. I spoke about our two minute walk across the lawn, because that was really the only memory we shared together. The very last thing I spoke about was the fact that Lenny was mine. That part, I do remember.

And finally, Lenny was my property. My only property. Nothing in the step-house was mine. Not the food or furniture or yard. Not the dog or even the bed. It's all step. I sleep in the step-bed, and eat at the step-table off of the step-plate under the step-grandmother's step-roof. Step, step, step. Lenny wasn't step-anything. He was my goat. And now he's gone.

I turned to the hole, Lenny's limp and bagged body lying beside it. I had never been to a funeral. I did what I thought felt appropriate. I rolled his body into the ground and began piling the shoveled dirt back into the hole, and I didn't pause even once until the last bit of Lenny's body bag was covered completely. When I finished, I stepped away from the mound. It formed a little hill, and I knew I could always find this burial spot, but Grandma's words lingered in me. Mark the spot. I ran back into the house and returned to the spot with Lenny's chain, the one he came with from Uncle Johnny. I stuck a part of it in the ground. Then I used the rest of the chain to form a heart. Figuring the heart would probably lose its shape thanks to the weather, I stuck tiny sticks in every other couple chain links so the shape would mostly remain.

Satisfied, I turned one last time to my invisible audience and sang a hymn. They probably sang hymns at funerals, whoever "they" is. I chose the only song I knew by heart from children's church, and that was "Jesus Loves Me." Usually we sang the chorus twice, meaning we sang the "Yes, Jesus loves me," part six times, but by the third time, I felt that the song was inappropriate. Lenny was dead. Reminding him that Jesus loved *me* wasn't very nice. Jesus understood.

That night, lying in the step-bed along with my mother and father, I heard weird noises. It must have been my imagination, I thought. It had to be. The noise was as though something soft was sliding against the ground, against the grass outside. Then I heard a loud bark, but it lowered into low barks and finally nothing at all. Butch must have been rolling around. That's what I assumed. I assumed Butch woke up suddenly and shifted around, trying to find a better position before falling asleep. I assumed that the sound of chains clinking together was Butch's chains, and the soft sound of metal against dirt was nothing.

Thump.

The sound was so familiar that I couldn't make up another cause for the noise except that of my goat hitting the ground. Then metal against dirt. Then crunches of grass being stepped on. I jerked my head up and crawled off the bed. Before I could make it to the door, my shirt was being grabbed from behind. I immediately stopped moving.

"Ronnie?"

It was Dad.

"Ronnie, get back in bed."

I think Grandma moved Lenny. I think she moved Lenny underneath Butch.

"She probably has her reasons. Get back in bed. It's late."

I nodded and followed Dad back into bed. I didn't motion to pull the covers over my body, not even to cover my feet. Mum was still sleeping. I didn't have to look. She was snoring straight into the pillow. I knew Dad wasn't asleep yet, though. He always took a while to sleep. That night, I was having trouble, too. It wasn't the thought of Grandma coming out in the middle of the night and disrespecting my burial that bothered me. Nor was it the actual image of her stealing a dead goat from its burial spot and burying him under the feet of his killer. What was haunting me was a different noise. The sound of a goat bleating. Or a child screaming. It sounded the same to

34

me. When I had met Lenny, he sounded like a little boy shrieking, like what my cousin Julian sounded like when Uncle Joe tossed him into the lake to teach him how to swim.

Daddy? You awake?

"Of course I am."

Do you hear that?

The bleating noise was really quiet, but right in my ear.

"Hear what, Ronnie?"

The bleating noise started up again, still soft.

That.

"Sounds like a kid screaming. It's real far, Ronnie, don't worry about it."

Even though Mum always slept between us, I could tell he turned away from me, facing the window. All I saw was a small part of the back of his head.

He was right. Through the window, there was a kid screaming, somewhere far beneath Butch's feet. I began to imagine that the kid was me. And, through the wall by my head, there was an old woman sitting in a white plastic deck chair with her lips curled up toward her brown, dark eyes. Alone.

The Virus

It was called "morning sickness." That was what Dad had been telling me every time I went to brush my teeth and found Mum tossing up dinner in the toilet. I figured that she had a tummy virus, because not only was she throwing up often, her stomach poked out more than usual. It wasn't a soft jelly poke, either. It was firm and stiff, as I imagined only a virus would do.

Also, it had to be a virus, because Dad had been pretty angry about it. Especially the day the virus had been discovered. I wasn't actually there. Mum and Dad were in the bedroom, speaking in low voices. I had known better than to eavesdrop – when they spoke all husky, it meant I wasn't supposed to be listening – but Dad's voice gradually became louder and louder, and I was forced into doing so.

"I thought you did!"

"I didn't, woman, I didn't!"

"As the man, you should have been considerate and do it, Sean!"

"As the woman, you should have been considerate and remind me to do it, Kim!"

Then their voices were low again, but that hadn't lasted long. It went right back to the shouting I couldn't have avoided listening to. Even if I tried.

"What are we supposed to do now, Kim? We'll have to wait almost another year before we can get out of this f-"

The voices disappeared one more time for good. I knew it was because Mum had shushed him. She always did that any time he raised his voice too loud. Sometimes he didn't listen, but in that particular time, he did.

It was about a month later when Mum started vomiting and feeling dizzy. I didn't have much time to be worried about Mum today, though. Tamika invited me over her house to play, and Marissa would be there too. This would be my second time at Tamika's house, and she said she received a gift she wanted to show us – well, me, because Marissa already saw it before. I had been at a funeral.

Just after patting Mum on the back as a good-bye, I spotted Dad in the bathroom doorway. His face always looked strange when he watched Mum hunched over the toilet, a mix of guilt in his soft eyebrows and irritation in his tight frown. As I passed by him, he placed a hand on my shoulder as the other rubbed against his forehead like he was trying to clean something off of it.

Yes, Dad?

"Pray for your mother, okay?"

I stared at him before offering a nod.

"Pray it out of her. Pray it out of her *soon*."

I nodded again and dashed out of the step-house.

Tamika's house was cozy, to say the least. It was bigger than Grandma's house, most definitely. Instead of two bedrooms, it had three, and it also had a basement. Hardly anyone around here had a basement. The first time I went to Tamika's house she had shown it to me. It was dark and smelled like dead rats drenched in paint. That day I had vowed never to step foot in a basement again. Thankfully we were planning on playing in the living room. That was where she said the gift was.

In front of the couch Marissa and I were sitting on stood Tamika, her chocolate puffy hair tied lazily into a bun on the back of her head. Every time Marissa or I tried to glance at the television, Tamika would pounce and get in the way.

"Nuh uh, no peekin'."

Marissa elbowed me. "I already know what it is, Tamika. Don't be stupid."

But I don't know-

"Ever heard of Nintendo, Ronnelle?"

"Marissa!"

I shook my head quickly. No. Maybe. What is it?

Tamika shoved her hand over Marissa's mouth and my line of vision was clear. In front of the television set there was a weird grey box, and in front of that was an even littler grey box with arrows and two red buttons. On the screen was something I had never seen before. A bunch of perfect squares of peach, red, and a puke green stacked to look like a tiny man with a hat and overalls. And a moustache. My instinct had been to laugh because it was cute.

"What? You have something better?" Tamika whined and crawled over to the boxes. "I try to show you my gift from Daddy and you laugh just like Marissa did!"

I stopped laughing. He's so funny looking and small. A baby man.

"Fine, he's funny looking, but he's good at jumpin' and savin' his girlfriend!" Tamika squealed. She picked up the smaller box. Her thumbs positioned over the arrows and the red buttons. I heard a click and the little man began to walk forward toward what looked like an angry mushroom. I didn't know what to think. This was a gift from her dad? Back in my old house, the gifts I got from Dad were either more chickens or new gloves for all the tree-climbing I did in the bush.

"It's called a Nintendo Entertainment System." Marissa pointed at the big grey box. Then her finger jutted towards the screen. "This game is *Super Mario Bros.* It's really popular. My big brother got it for his birthday."

And for the rest of the afternoon, the three of us took turns completing levels in the game, all the while snacking on the bowl of kurma Tamika's dad had set out on the table. It was nice. We did that for a few Fridays and Saturdays. Sometimes Tamika's older brother would help us with the harder parts. He would steal some of our sweets and we'd chase him around the couch. Having a brother seemed really cool.

Meanwhile at home, the virus in Mum was getting bigger to the point where I felt too bad to leave the house to play *Mario.* So, one Saturday, I decided to stay home. Mum was sprawled across the bed, arms stretched and mouth wide open with groans spilling out of it. It was scary.

Mummy, are you dying?

"Just the opposite, actually," she hooted.

What does that mean?

"I have no idea. Get me a hot wet rag and a bar of soap. The one that smells like cinnamon."

I came back with the things she asked for, and to my utter shock, she held the soap up to her mouth.

Are you gonna eat that, Mummy? To clean your insides or somethin'?

"Oo, that'd be nice."

"Kim!" Dad barged in. "Kim! Get that damn soap away from your mouth!" Dad snatched the soap away from her and tossed it into the big blanket that was all bunched up from supporting Mum's back the night before.

"I just love the smell of it, Sean. I wasn't going to try to eat it this time," Mum snapped. And then she giggled.

I turned to Dad, because Mum didn't seem like the most reliable source. Is Mummy dying?

He didn't say anything. He just blinked.

I glanced back at Mum.

"You didn't tell the poor child, Sean?"

He slowly shook his head, but his eyes were completely absent. "I thought I – I've been so distracted with the papers and the job I-"

Papers. I always heard that word being thrown around by Dad, and sometimes by Mum, and I was beginning to get really tired of it. It seemed to be linked to every major problem we had as a family. I didn't know what it meant. And at that point, I didn't care. I didn't know which paper to hate, so I went safe and decided to hate them all.

Tell me now! I yelled.

That was out of line. I prepared myself for a good whack on the arm, but nothing came down on me. I opened my eyes and Dad and Mum were staring. Mum glared at Dad. He sighed.

"Ronnie, I'm sorry. Relax yourself," he told me. He reached his hand out and I cringed in fear, but all he did was rest his hand on my shoulder. He sat me down on the bed.

Is Mummy dying? I asked again. Is the virus getting worse?

"No, Ronnie. I told you to relax. I know it's been sounding like she has, but what's happening right now is a good thing." He looked at Mum and took her hand. "A really good thing. It's not a virus. It's a gift."

Oddly enough, the first thing I thought of when I heard "gift" was a Nintendo Entertainment System. I thought maybe my parents wanted to distract me with a NES, and I was unfortunately okay with that at the time. But I was terribly, terribly wrong. And stupid – we had no television set anyhow.

My head was spinning. At some point in Dad's speech of hardship and struggle, two words stuck out: papers *and* baby. He didn't explain anything about the papers. In fact, he hardly explained the baby portion, too. I could hardly remember what exactly he said, but I was conscious enough to put the pieces together.

Mum wasn't sick. She had no virus, but there was a living thing inside her. A baby. And this "baby" posed some sort of conflict with the "papers." I didn't know how to feel. Having a sibling seemed like fun according to my times with Tamika's brother, but now with the association between the baby and the papers, I felt a strange feeling against both.

Mum was scanning my face. She looked like she wanted to cry. "A-are you alright, Ronnie?"

I nodded. I'm fine, Mummy.

Dad looked relieved. "I wish I took it as well as she did."

"I told you she would."

And they hugged me. Mum's stiff stomach dug into my side, but I kept my lips in a tight smile. So tight that it hurt.

We had many moments as a family. We were small to begin with, and being stuffed in the same room really forced us to pay attention to each other. It had always been the three of us. The step-house changed that. It would be the three of us, and now, a virus.

A virus that would just grow and grow.

Rotten Mangoes

The virus, as I assumed, did not get any better. *Bigger* is not better. It caused Mum's stomach to expand so much it looked like there was a football under all the clothes she wore. Speaking of her clothes, all she wore those days were big loose house dresses that fit like curtains. She said it was more comfortable, but I thought it was because she was trying to hide the fat. And that fat didn't feel like fat at all. Fat was supposed to be squishy and soft. Mum's stomach was hard. It was hard and when I hugged her before bed, because lately she had been insisting on goodnight hugs, her stomach would jab me in the ribs. It hurt. I didn't say anything since she always looked like she was on the verge of tears. I'd cry too if there were a boulder in my stomach.

She threw up many times over the next couple months. I'd wake up and both she and Dad would be gone. Then I'd go to the bathroom and there they'd be: Mum hunched over the toilet, and Dad with his fingers pinching his forehead. Then his nose.

"Sean, it's killing me!" Mum said one time.

"It'll be over in a few months, honey."

From that moment, I felt as though I wasn't the only one in the step-house who believed this thing truly was a virus. Actually, I had always known Grandma didn't like it. She wasn't exactly subtle about her feelings. Sometime she'd walk by the bathroom, take a whiff of the vomit scent in the air, and mumble something. *Another mouth to feed.* That was my favorite one – she never fed *us*.

During the final months of the virus, I went back to going to Tamika's house for play dates. We played her NES as usual, but something I began to really take an interest in was her older brother. Adam. He was sixteen and he looked like a pole bean. Long and skinny. He introduced us to this other game, *The Legend of Zelda*, but the music was creepy and there weren't many bright colors. I didn't like it. Neither did Marissa and Tamika. What I did like, though, was watching him play it. He looked so determined, and he beat the little armored enemies much faster than I did. I also liked when he chased us around the table or stole our candy. I hoped he thought of me like a sister. He always ruffled my curls when he walked by with his stick legs.

One day he busted through the door and met us in the living room with his white teeth gleaming. Tamika called him stupid, but he ignored it and asked if I wanted to come pick mangoes with him.

Me?

"Yeah. You said you grew up in the bush, right? Shimmying up trees is nothing for you," he replied.

And for the first time, something strange happened with the temperature of my cheeks. I told the girls I'd be right back and ran after Adam to their backyard. I knew the family grew mangoes in their backyard, but I never thought I'd be able to help pick them. Adam handed me a wooden bucket and we stood at the base of one tree. Then he grabbed this metal rod from the grass and struck a lower branch. Four mangoes fell. I was able to catch two of them in the bucket, and he caught the other two with his hand.

"There's a trick to it." Adam chuckled and tossed the others in my bucket.

We retrieved all the lower ones first – the ones that could be caught by using the rod. Then it was climbing time. Adam was able to prop himself right onto the intersection of branches. I dropped the bucket on the grass. He reached his hand out and helped me up. Then he was off. He climbed up the thick branches as if they were nothing. I took a moment to pull my gloves on (I carried them everywhere) and climbed a different branch. Together we tossed down the mangoes into the bucket below. I accidentally smashed a few of them on the ground, but for the most part, the mangoes weren't damaged. Adam maneuvered through the branches like a monkey, and when I pointed it out, we both started to laugh. Then we both made monkey noises. It was the most fun I'd had in a long time. Romping around in the trees – it reminded me of home. My new friends at school didn't live near big bush and they weren't as into climbing as I was. Even though this wasn't bush, for just a second it was home.

"Okay, monkey, let's go." Adam jumped off the branch and sunk into his knees so it wouldn't hurt so much. My dad had taught me to do that before. So, I did the same, except I had to tuck and roll, too.

We inspected the bucket. Adam grabbed and lightly squeezed each mango. They were a soft orange that melted into a bright yellow. Perfectly ripe. He suddenly tossed me one.

"Adam's Mangoes," he stated and sunk his teeth into the one in his hand. He spit the skin off and ate the meat.

I smiled and ate mine. It was delicious. It beat kurma and candy by far. We then threw the pits onto the grass and walked back to the house. Adam let me keep four of them, one for everyone at the step-house. It was supposed to include Grandma, but I figured Mum needed an additional mango for all her trouble. And I didn't want Grandma to have one.

When I entered the house that late afternoon with the four mangoes in a little burlap sack Adam lent me, Mum was standing in the kitchen resting her hands on her thighs as if she were recovering from squats. I called out from the door, my feet glued to where I stood. She grunted in response. As if on cue, Dad came out from our bedroom with a damp rag and a cell phone by his ear.

"I called Gary. He's going to bring his maxi. Should be here in a second, Kim. Just breathe," he told Mum. He held up the rag for her and she bit it. She shut her eyes.

After this point, everything was in slow motion. There was a car horn blasting outside. Dad grabbed Mum's arm and hobbled her out of the step-house. Mum's hand smacked my sack of mangoes. It was involuntary, because her eyelids were still pressed together like the sun was beaming on them. My mangoes fell onto the wooden floor and rolled toward the kitchen. I motioned to retrieve them, but Dad barked at me to stop my bacchanal and come outside. I hesitated.

Grandma emerged from her own bedroom. Her beady eyes went wide, not when she spotted my mum in pain, but when she spotted my mangoes on her floor. Before she could bend over and grab them, I screamed they were mine. Mine.

"You think I'll leave it just so? Stop your gun talk – I'll keep them in a safe place."

Grandma was a long eye, someone who liked things that aren't their property. I felt doltish for accepting her words, but as time sped up, I lost the ability to think. Dad grabbed me by the collar of my tank top and pushed me into the maxi.

And time continued to crawl and fly and crawl and fly to the point where I couldn't tell what day it was. Throughout that week, I was thrown all over the place. Into a maxi taxi. Out of a maxi taxi. Into a small hospital with four doctors and ten nurses. In and out of a waiting room. In a little hallway with a window that allowed me to see my Mum – or, really, her feet, because the bed had a curtain surrounding most of it. When I got jittery, I was thrown into a little playroom with wooden blocks and hand-sewn dolls. When I got hungry, I was thrown into the tiny white room they called the cafeteria.

Finally, when I got quiet, I was thrown into Mum's room. She was lying in her mint bed, feet still exposed. In her arms was a rolled blue blanket. I knew what was in it. I saw the outline of its circular head.

"Why are you standing so far away, Ronnie? Come look at your new brother," Mum whispered.

I allowed myself to look at her face. Her skin was flushed and pasty, something people like us never really witnessed since we were all caramel and beaten by the sun all year. Her long, thick black hair looked greasy. Sweaty. Under her eyes were little smiles, but not the good kind. They were the kind that show up when you're really tired.

Mum?

"Come, Ronnie. Don't look at me like I'm an alien." Mum's shoulders bumped up and down – I think she was laughing, but no noise came out of her mouth.

I stepped closer by her command, rounding the bed to get a better view of her face. Dad stood on the other side of the bed, brushing his fingers through Mum's hair and smiling down at the thing in the blanket.

"You haven't even looked at the baby once," Dad pointed out with a frown.

"He's beautiful, ent?" Mum asked me.

But now you're not.

"Dammit, child. Look at the boy. Give him a chance," Dad said. He squinted at me and I knew if I said anything else without thinking, I'd get it.

So, I made a big show of leaning over the bed and studying the virus wrapped in the blanket. Its face was round and all the features were pudgy and undefinable. It had little bits of dark hair on its head. Its eyes were closed shut.

Then I looked at Mum, and her eyes had slowly come to a close as well. Time was slow again. Dad moved his fingers from Mum's head to the virus's head. Its fleshy nose twitched for a moment. For some reason, that made Dad smile.

"It's okay, Brendan. It's just Daddy," Dad murmured. He retracted his hand.

Brendan?

"Yes. That's his name. Go ahead and touch him."

I shook my head. I didn't want to. I was afraid of Brendan. I was afraid of how he connected to the papers. I was afraid of what he did to Mum. I was afraid of how he looked like no one and everyone at the same time.

"He's just a baby."

I didn't move.

And then he said something that made me remember why I always listened to him.

"Meeting a new sibling is like walking on the beach at noon. The sand is hot at first. It burns. You pick up your feet longer to fight the pain, and try to find shadows of the grass to escape the heat." He placed his hand back on the baby's head. "But then you remember that the sand is so hot because the sun is at its highest. And you remember that you're on a beach. A beach. What's a beach without hot sand? So what do you do?"

Nothing came to mind.

"You keep walking."

I did not obey Dad because he always had a belt ready, although that did help often. I obeyed Dad because he was a writer. Because the things he said on occasions where I needed them most, sunk into parts of my brain that everyday life couldn't ever touch. Dad painted pictures with words. He was the smartest man I knew. Did I understand his metaphor? No. But I could infer what he meant.

I stuck my hand out and rested it on Brendan's head. I wanted to say something, like hello, but I thought that'd be pointless. He was a baby. Would he recall my voice? Did it matter right now?

"Introduce yourself," Mum suddenly said, her eyes opening, but not all the way.

I looked at Brendan. The longer I had my hand against his light skin, the more I wished to cry.

I'm Ronnelle, but you can call me Ronnie, I whispered. Okay?

Maybe I spoke louder than I thought, or maybe Brendan knew he was being spoken to. Either way, I felt a ping in my chest when his eyes fluttered open and glossed over my face with little focus. I took it as his way of saying okay.

After that, Mum needed just a few more days of rest with Brendan. Dad and I slept at the hospital. It was small and not very busy, so the nurses encouraged us to stay. Plus it had air conditioning. Apparently Brendan was underweight, but that was solved soon because by the end of the week we were all back in the step-house.

And, of course, Grandma had eaten every single mango.

Message Received

I'm not quite sure why I had thought my brother would be just like Adam, Tamika's brother. Adam was sixteen; Brendan hadn't been alive before Sunday. Adam looked like a healthy pole bean; Brendan looked like a fleshy doll. Adam could climb trees and make monkey noises; Brendan could only stick his hand in his mouth and cry.

Cry. That's all he did. He didn't smile or laugh or do anything except cry. I never saw Adam cry. Mum and Dad seemed to crawl towards insanity each night we tried to get some sleep. Barely two hours could go by and Brendan would snap. I thought maybe it was the fact that he had to sleep on a couch cushion on the floor that made him cry, but Mum insisted he was only hungry and she flung her shirt above her collarbone and began to breastfeed.

Hungry? You mean thirsty?

"I mean, if milk is the only thing that you can consume, then it's quenching thirst and hunger, right?" Mum laughed.

Mum was constantly trying to be funny, too. Either that, or she was going so crazy that she laughed at everything she said.

"Come on, baby, don't cry. If one runs out, I've got another right here." Cue laughter.

"I would sing a lullaby to calm you down but that'll probably make you cry even more, huh?" Cue laughter.

"There there, Brendan. Stop screaming, you'll wake up Grandma and her late night visitor." Cue laughter.

"It's really early in the morning, but I'll see what we have in stock." Cue tears.

If she wasn't laughing, she was crying. If she wasn't crying, she was just dead silent with an angry baby.

Dad noticed Mum's growing hysteria. He must have. He was a writer, so things couldn't go unnoticed. I knew he knew the disturbance this baby was causing, but he never talked about it. He let it happen. I hated it. He caught me staring at Brendan napping once. I must have been making a face because he said if I frowned any harder my cheeks would snap. Then he brought up the beach again.

"Hot sand." He placed his finger on Brendan's forehead. "But when he's sleeping, we're standing in the shade."

He smiled at me as if that'd make me feel better. As if to smack Dad in the face, Brendan woke up and began shrieking again. At the time, Mum was in the living room resting on the couch (even though a cushion was missing, we still used it). I was about to dart out of the bedroom to get away from the noise when Dad told me to stop. I dragged my foot and faced him. He had Brendan in his arms, bopping up and down like he was listening to calypso.

"Take him with you."

I opened my mouth to say something, but what was there to say? The thing is, I had never held Brendan, not once. I had barely even touched him since he was born. We may have had a moment in the hospital, but frankly, I wasn't interested in having another. Brendan was whiny. Needy. I hardly asked for anything from my parents. Brendan seemed the opposite. He was too soft.

But my body moved against the will of my brain and I found myself holding Brendan against my torso, his circle head leaning on my shoulder. At first, he was still. His crying melted into little squeaky grunts, and I almost found it cute. Then he realized he wasn't doing his job, and he went straight back to screaming again. He wiggled weakly.

"Get him to Mum, Ronnie," Dad said. His eyebrows twitched. He regretted letting me hold the baby.

I left the bedroom and took the short trip to the living room. I couldn't see Mum's head peeking from the couch, so I went around it to see if she was lying down. She wasn't there. Brendan's screaming made my left ear throb. I wanted to just drop him and run away.

My search wasn't long. I spotted Mum in the kitchen, her hands balled up in fists and locked on her hips. It was her all-jokes-aside stance. Anytime Mum was angry at me and she made a little joke about the situation, right after it she'd stand in that very stance to show that she was serious. I stepped a little closer to the scene, now noticing Grandma on her knees, searching through a lower cupboard. It was odd. Mum and Grandma never stood in the same room if they could avoid it.

Mu-

"I swear if I have to hear that damn baby cry one more time I'm kicking him out of the house!" Grandma yelled, halfway in the cabinet by now. They haven't noticed me yet.

"Don't call him a *damn* baby!" Mum retorted. "Don't call him anything! You think I'm not tired of the crying too, Ma?"

"I'm doing you a favor." Grandma leaned away from the cupboard and looked up at Mum. "Now do me a favor and shut up that damn baby."

Mum held up her hand and for just a moment I thought she was going to hit Grandma across the face. But I knew Mum. And Mum knew herself. So she didn't. And that was when I realized just how much she loved Brendan. Brendan with his little eyes and little head. Brendan who looked like nothing.

"Ronnelle?"

I looked away from the baby to Mum. She sighed and pressed her hand to her forehead as if she were checking for a fever.

"I'm sorry you..." She trailed off. *I'm sorry you had to hear that.*

I nodded. I hadn't even noticed Brendan had stopped crying already. When Mum reached her arms out toward me, I held up Brendan to her. To my surprise, she looped her arms around me instead.

Mummy?

Mum pulled away, snapped out of a trance. She took Brendan from me and rested his head on her shoulder. "Just a little more time and we're out of here," she said to Brendan. Or to me. I wasn't sure.

I wanted to ask what she meant, but then there was the satisfying sound of Grandma slamming her bedroom door. She didn't like when we had our little family moments. Sometimes I felt bad for her – maybe she felt left out – but I'd get over it because there was a reason she felt left out. A very legitimate reason that was entirely her fault.

The following days went by a little differently than before. I'd head to school by myself since Mum was too busy to walk me. Dad still went to work while Mum stayed home with Grandma and Brendan. After school I had used to hang out with Tamika and Marissa around the grounds and then we'd take our time walking home together, but now I sped home. It must be scary to be home alone with Grandma so often. I had to keep Mum company. At home, I'd do my homework and orbit around Mum in case she needed anything. The longer I stuck around Mum and the baby, the more I understood why Dad and Mum bothered to keep him. Sure, he cried about everything, but Dad was right. When he was sleeping or eating or lying silently on the bed watching us, we were standing in the shade.

What really won me over was one Saturday morning. Once again I had declined Tamika's invitation to play NES with her, Marissa, and Adam. I told Mum she could lay down and take a nap while I watched Brendan. She didn't even wait for me to change my mind – she fell right back in bed with a sigh. I took Brendan into the living room and plopped myself onto the couch, cradling him on my lap. I sat for a while, just enjoying the calm, when I heard the front door click.

"Your mummy taking a break?" Grandma asked as she walked into the house with a paper bag in her hand. It was greasy at the bottom. Looked like she bought pholourie.

Taking in the sweet and spicy smell of chutney and fried dough balls, I closed my eyes and leaned my head back onto the couch, my thumb drawing little circles on Brendan's back.

"You want one, ent?"

My eyes shot open. There were rare occasions where Grandma dropped microscopic signs that she had a heart. I looked back to the kitchen, trying to peek my head over the couch as much as possible, and nodded quickly.

Grandma opened up the paper bag on the counter. A white container popped out, along with a tiny plastic bowl filled with the chutney. She opened both and held up a single ball. Her arm swung back and forth, preparing to toss it in my direction. I reached out my hand, ready to catch. I was always good at catching.

But Grandma didn't throw it. She just dipped it in the sauce and stuffed it in her mouth, and through her oiled teeth, she said, "I already give you people a house and a room and a couch and a floor and a roof and a yard. A place to walk around that's not outside. You want to take my food, too?"

I retracted my hand and placed it back underneath Brendan's legs. I didn't want to be in her line of vision anymore. I didn't want to be in the same room. I motioned towards the bedroom, but there was a sudden gagging noise. I jumped, my eyes shooting back to my grandmother. Her hands were cupped around her throat and her eyes bulged out from their sockets. She was choking.

The best part, of course, was when I looked down. Brendan was smiling. A twinkle in his brown eyes. A toothless grin. I felt a blanket of warmth wrap around my entire body. He was smiling at Grandma, or, at least, what was happening to her.

And as quickly as the choking began, it had concluded. After a few quick coughs and a sip of water from the pipe, Grandma was fine. I hadn't moved a centimeter.

"What you stickin' for?" Grandma yelled. Another cough. "Go to the room, nah!"

I giggled and ducked straight into the bedroom. She was humiliated.

That same night, I was lying in bed with Brendan tucked under my hand. We were having a staring contest. While he wasn't good at keeping his eyes on one object, he was good at keeping them wide open. Brendan won his third game when I heard a slam from outside the bedroom. I leaped off the bed, glancing back at Brendan to make sure he was still lying there, and pressed my ear against the door.

The sound of Dad's dressy work shoes tapping the ground. Mum's bare feet patting the kitchen tile. A hand slamming the counter. Angry voices.

"Devil baby!" Grandma's voice. Undoubtedly.

A mixture of Mum's light, singsong voice and Dad's low one.

I wrapped my fingers around the doorknob and twisted it all the way around. Then I pushed the door open, just a crack. Just enough that I could see the window in the living room. I pictured Dad and Mum standing on one side of the kitchen counter, and Grandma on the other side, by herself.

"I'm done with her, Sean! Done!" Mum.

"What you callin' my child a devil baby for?" Dad.

"You know what he did today? I choke on my pholourie and the boy was smiling and cackling and having a blast!"

That was a bit dramatic. There was silence. I imagined my parents stifling laughter. I knew they would have enjoyed that moment.

"He's two months, Ma. He don't know what he's doing!" Dad had gotten serious again.

"He hasn't even laughed yet," Mum added.

"Well *someone* laughed real hard. Devil child!"

"Stop that nonsense, Ma!" Mum. "Ronnie's just a kid."

"Yeah, and she's my grandchild, ent? I don't want any grandchild of mine to act so."

I swallowed. That was the first time Grandma ever established we were related. That I was hers. I stepped away from the door to check on Brendan again. Through all the noise, he was fast asleep. He was lucky, not knowing about any of the anger flooding the step-house. I pulled the thin bed sheet over his body and moved back to the door. But the sound of Mum's feet slapping the ground and Dad's shoes clicking get louder and louder, and I dove onto the bed.

The door swung open, lifting Grandma's hollers.

"-out! I want you out!"

And the door closed.

Mummy?

Mum and Dad looked to each other, and then to me.

I want to get out of here.

"Then let's go. Gary's waiting out front."

I thought they were joking. We didn't use Gary all that often, only for emergencies like when Mum's water broke. He was a maxi driver, and typically maxis followed main roads and let people in and out by stops, but because Gary "owed Dad a favor," we could call him and have him get off course to directly pick us up. I let my head fall back onto the pillow and shut my eyes, but Mum flicked the layer of fat under my chin.

"Did you hear your father? We're leaving."

But her voice didn't sound sad. Or disappointed. Or even angry. I watched her pull out two avocado green suitcases from under the bed. She let out a grunt as she lifted them up. They were already packed. Dad took them from her and opened the closet we all shared. Some of my clothes were still in it. He threw them into a suitcase and zipped it up. It was funny. We didn't have much to pack. The larger suitcase had all of our clothes stuffed in it. The smaller one had other supplies and Brendan's baby things. A pacifier. A couple stuffed toys and blankets. His spare cloth diaper.

And just like the hospital escapade, things were swapping between slow motion and fast forward. We were packed in a flash. We were out of the bedroom. But actually exiting the step-house seemed like an eternity. Within that time, I placed *Til the Well Runs Dry* on the couch for Grandma to read on the nights her friend couldn't sleep over. Mum and Dad were already out the door. I pecked Brendan on the forehead and looked back at Grandma leaning over the kitchen island Grandpa had built years before I was born. She watched me. I held her gaze.

One of the biggest dilemmas I ever had to face as a kid moving from the step-house was whether I should have waved good-bye to my grandmother or not. I know the night I buried Lenny in the backyard, she told me to mark the spot so she could find him and move the body to rest underground beneath Butch. I know when I spied on her that one evening to see if she had a television, she knew I was there, and she didn't say anything. I know she told me it didn't matter where our money was coming from because she didn't want me to be concerned about how much we were making, or how we were even making it. I know she ate all my mangoes because there wasn't much to eat in her house in the first place. I know, until we moved in, she never locked her front door. I know she was lonely.

I always knew she was lonely.

And I always knew she didn't like me. I knew she didn't like Brendan. I knew she didn't like Mum, or even Dad, or anyone in my family. In this way, I supposed, she would get what she wanted. To be alone. To not be surrounded by people who fell into her life only because she loved Grandpa later than his first wife did.

Thus, when Grandma broke the stare and tossed me the last of her pholourie, I caught it with my left hand and threw it right back. And when I looked down at my little brother, he was smiling with ignorant bliss, looking directly at Grandma.

Grandma told us to go.

So we did.

Part One and a Half

Midway

Plain Ride

You would think entering an airport and getting in a plane and even flying in a plane would be the most chilling childhood experience, but oddly enough, I hardly remember any of it. I was nine by that time. I should have been excited. But instead, my mind was racing about other things. Grandma. I figured she would be happy that we were gone, but I wondered if that was what she really wanted. Anytime I finished a book, I saw things a little differently. Dad had always told me that that was the point. *'Til the Well Runs Dry* did its job. People don't always express what they want. Sometimes they did the opposite of what they want, actually. Did Grandma do the same?

The airport was nothing special. I had been to it before, but usually just to welcome family back home. While we waited for the scheduled time, Mum bought us chicken and chips from one of the vendors. We ate. We were called. We boarded the plane. Mum sat next to me. Brendan was in her arms. Dad sat on the opposite row. At some point I was offered water. I took it. I drank it.

The lift was somewhat fun. I felt my stomach drop and my ears got cloggy. Once we reached the top and leveled off, Mum told me to pinch my nose, shut my mouth, and try to breathe out so my ears popped. I got the window seat, so I was able to look outside. The clouds were nice to watch. I was never so close to them before. From the ground, the sky looked like someone just painted the clouds on it. Like it was two-dimensional. But being in a plane, it surrounded us, and the clouds even shook the plane when we flew through them. They were real.

Eventually the clouds bored me and I closed my eyes. I took lots of naps. I had lots of little dreams. Dreams about Lenny and me playing tag in the backyard. About jumping on the bed with Brendan, even though he was still an infant. About eating pholourie with Grandma. The weirdest part was that all of them took place at the step-house. Not my old house with the garden and the chickens and the sliding back door and my own room, but the step-house with the angry dog chained up outside and the dead goat buried under him and the one couch in the living room. It made me sad.

We stopped at some point during the flight. Captain said it was time to refuel. I didn't find it interesting, and I asked Mum how long the trip was going to be. She said a number, but it came out more like a breath of air. Then she fell asleep. Brendan happily slept through a good portion of the flight. He wasn't so interested in the ride, just like me. Dad's knee was shaking up and down each time I woke up. Maybe he was thinking about Grandma, too. The sky began to make me feel sick, and I pulled the window shade down.

Every now and then, when Mum turned her attention away from Brendan and to me, she'd suggest games for us to play to pass the time. We played I-Spy, but I got flustered and ended up spying the same set of things each turn. So we gave up with the games and just decided to sleep.

Then the pilot announced for us to prepare for landing. This time, it was, as he joked, the "real deal." I didn't know what that meant, so I sat up a little straighter. Then there was a tug in my stomach and my ears felt funny. Brendan's face was threatening to cry, but Mum calmed him down. Dad rubbed his hands against his thighs over and over again. I could feel the plane wheels smack the ground, and I remembered that I should have been looking out the window. When I moved the shade, all there was to see was long strips of road for the planes to land and lift off from. I should have opened the window sooner. Despite all the naps I took, I was especially sleepy when we came to a stop. We grabbed our stuff, which wasn't much in the first place, and exited the plane, following the people in front of us.

The most distinct memory I have of the plane ride was when we were walking through the tunnel to leave the plane. It finally occurred to me that I didn't know where we were. I looked up at Dad, squeezing his sweaty hand.

Dad?

"Yes, Ronnie?"

Where are we?

"Get ready for those streets of gold, baby girl."

And I remembered the last words to Mrs. Sadd's little jingle – the words I had forgotten before.

58

Part Two

New Country

The Motel Room

The new airport didn't look too different from the one back home. It felt so odd to be in one place one night, and then the next morning you're in a completely different country. I was sick to my stomach. Mum offered me a bottle of water she bought from one of the vendors, and I grabbed it and chugged it down. She left me on the bench with our suitcases piled by my feet while she took Brendan to a quiet corner to feed him. Dad had disappeared for a while. He said, not to me, that he had to go talk to "the man." Who "the man" was, I didn't know, but when Dad mentioned he had something to do with the papers, I immediately didn't like the man. I didn't like the man at all. Alone on the bench, I quickly drifted off to sleep.

When I woke up, I was lying across a thin bed with a really thick blanket and plain white pillows on it. Mum was sprawled across another bed about a meter away, Brendan lying beside her. And, of course, Dad was nowhere to be seen again. I wiped my eyes and found a little clock on the nightstand between the beds. It was three in the afternoon. I yawned.

And then it hit me again. Where were we? Was *this* our new home? I didn't see any kitchen or dining room or living room. In fact, the only door, beside the front door, was the door to a bathroom with a broken showerhead and plastic curtains. I frowned. This couldn't be our new home. I spotted a window and ran for it, flinging the curtains to the side. Our home had a poor view of power lines and a McDonald's across the road.

Streets of gold, I can finally see.

My eyes focused on the street. It was certainly not gold. It was a mouse gray. Cracked. The only thing remotely close to gold was the yellow line streaked across the center that divided the road. My eyes stung, and I knew it wasn't because of all the sunlight beaming through the room. Everyone lied. Everyone had lied to me. The streets weren't gold.

Well, at least, *those* streets weren't gold. Maybe we weren't there yet. The longer I stood there, the more I began to realize that our home looked more like a hotel room then an actual place to live, and relief flooded over me. I pulled the window open and a sudden gust of wind smacked me in the face. I was shocked. My skin flipped over itself, and I rubbed my arms up and down to create heat. As fast as I opened that window, I closed it. The air here was as unwelcoming as the streets. Shuddering, I turned back to my little brother and Mum. The cold must have woken her, because she was already sitting straight up with her hands grasping her arms, just like I had been a few seconds ago.

Mummy, where are we?

She yawned and rubbed Brendan's head of itty bitty curls. "We're in a motel, Ronnie."

Where's Dad?

"Right here!" The door that led outside flung open and out popped Dad with a large grocery bag in one hand. He slammed the door behind him. "And don't get too comfortable." He winked at Mum.

I never knew people winked in real life, but Dad did it at that moment and I wanted to laugh. Our suitcases were still fully packed and lying on the floor – of course we weren't staying for long.

Mum looked completely delighted. "You made the arrangements? We're all set?" She smiled over at me as if I would know what was going on.

Dad nodded and gave Brendan a kiss on the head. "It's an hour drive from here – she lives in the suburbs."

"The suburbs? Oh, well then that's perfect. A big city like Philadelphia will be too much for us," Mum replied. Brendan was beginning to make his soft mumbling noises. Mum picked him up, ready to feed him again.

Philadelphia?

Dad looked at me. "Yes. We're in *Philly*. Who knew we'd make it here?" He was so worked up. Dad didn't show all that much emotion, so at moments like these, I didn't know whether to be scared or excited. "Ms. Hurt lives alone and she gets off work today at about four. I picked up some maps." He tossed Mum and me a crumpled map from his pocket. "We have to take a taxi westward to the suburbs. It's real small. Shouldn't be too much of a change from home – what time is it?"

STREETS OF MELTED GOLD

I stared down at the map, tuning out Mum and Dad's voices. There were millions of different color lines. Blue. Black. Green. Red. I didn't understand any of it. I pushed the map closer to Mum and headed for the front door.

But both of them called out of my name. I turned around.

"Ronnie, get your tail back over here," Mum yelled.

Back home, I had always left the house without really letting anyone know. It had never been a problem. I slowly walked back to the bed and didn't say a word. Sometimes the best way to handle being scolded by my parents was to say absolutely nothing.

"This isn't like where we used to live, Ronnelle. We don't know anyone here. We don't know this neighborhood, this street, nothing. You do not just leave without permission," Dad explained, grasping his head.

How was I supposed to know? From what I saw through the window, the neighborhood wasn't anything new. Just colder. Tinted grey.

Sorry.

"It's okay, crapaud." Dad flung the plastic bag at the bed.

What's in there?

Mum laid Brendan on his back. He was awake, but he seemed content, and any time he was in that state of mind, we tried to prolong it as long as possible. The bag made whispering noises as she dug her hand through it. "Sweaters. It's real cold up here." She held up a black puffy jacket. I thought it was for her, but then she threw on to my lap.

For me?

"That's all yours, Ronnie," Dad chimed in. "Try it on."

He seemed happy. I pushed my arms through the soft, smooth sleeves and instantly felt warm. Really warm. There was no need for jackets back home. Wearing one now – it made me feel different. But, again, Dad was happy, and I put on my best Christmas smile.

"Gosh, Sean, it's a little big, ent?" Mum asked. She was completely right. The sleeves were so long you couldn't see the tips of my fingers. I didn't even have to look in a mirror to know that I looked like a pumped up beach ball.

Dad gave me a little push on the shoulder. "Of course, woman. I bought it a couple sizes bigger so she could grow into it. That thing'll last."

Mum rolled her eyes and smiled at me. One of those smiles she gave when she didn't really agree to what Dad was saying, but because he was Dad, she agreed to it anyways. Then she took out another jacket from the bag, except this one was tiny and absolutely perfect for Brendan. She laughed and began to put it on for him. It was an onesie stuffed with white fluff to keep him warm. There were ears on the top of the hood. He looked like a kitten. Mum said she wished she had a camera to take a picture of him.

It's your turn!

Mum and Dad looked at me, then at each other. They smiled and tried on their own new jackets. It almost felt like Christmas, except there was no pastelle and sorrel, and it was cold outside. Mum's jacket was light purple with feathery white fur around the hood and a matching white zipper. The jacket was long, ending at her mid-thigh. Dad's jacket was brown with a black patch on each elbow. It seemed like he had the thinnest coat out of all of us. When I asked him if it would keep him warm, he answered all cool and confident. "It's a *windbreaker*. Sounds like it'll do its job, right?"

It was all fun and games, strutting around in thick clothing we had never needed to wear before, but eventually Dad got serious again and emptied the rest of the grocery bag into one of our suitcases. I wasn't able to catch a glimpse of what they were, but I assumed it was other little things we needed.

And we were off again. A family on the move, as Dad had chanted. Threw on our shoes. Grabbed our suitcases. Left a key on the bed. We were out of the motel room.

The excitement was finally beginning to kick in.

Accents

The maxi taxi was much smaller than what I had been used to. Instead of it being a van that could easily fit eight people, this one fit only three in the back, and one in the passenger seat (but I doubt anyone would want to sit next to the driver). Brendan balanced easy on Mum's lap, I took the middle, and Dad was on the other side. I was disappointed considering I wanted to poke my head out the window and see everything. Feel the cold wind, even. They drove on the right side of the road here. I wanted to see everything. When I reached to roll the window down, Mum slapped my hand and asked if I was stupid.

Oh, gosh, Mummy!

Then the driver suddenly guffawed from the front seat and we all shot our eyes towards his dark reflection in the rearview mirror. His gaze met mine for a moment, but he seemed more focused to my right – where Mum was seated.

"I'm sorry, I just love the accent."

Accent? If anything, he had the accent. He enunciated every letter in every word. It took so long for him to say such a simple sentence, it exhausted me just listening to him. I remained quiet and looked at Dad. Then I leaned in and whispered.

The driver sounds like people you hear on the television.

Dad smirked. "'Cause most of that stuff on TV is shot here, baby girl," he replied.

All those TV shows were shot here in...what had Dad called it earlier? Philly? I was star struck. My arms began to itch. I wanted to meet someone famous, like the voice of Baby Ms. Piggy.

"So how long have you guys been here?" the driver asked.

Dad clenched his fist. "Long enough. We want to leave the city for something quieter."

"Right, right, for the kids."

The driver asked more questions, but I lost interest. I looked out the windshield since Mum's head was blocking the window to my right and Dad was half-way blocking the one to my left.

The buildings were gradually getting taller and closer together. There were traffic lights at every corner, and when I thought we were about to go for a smooth ride down the street, we stopped at another intersection. Sometimes we waited ages for the stoplight, because herds of people crossed the road at a time. Back home, we just made a run for it. Didn't need a white man to light up and tell us when it was safe to cross.

There was a mix between big businesses with huge lit up signs across the top and outlets with nothing but a funny yard sign taped to the window to tell you what store they were. The sidewalks were smothered with people of chocolate skin color at first, but as we drove further and further, I began to see more and more vanilla. Sure, I've seen many Blacks and Chinees and Indians back home – both of my parents were half Indian. Douglas, as they were called. I was one, too. Never in my life, though, had I seen people with eyes so open and skin so white.

I turned to Mum and asked if there wasn't much sun here. That had to be it. After all, the sun wasn't shining that bright, and the wind was cold. I supposed it made sense the people were lighter.

But Mum said they did get sun. Plenty of sun. "It's fall, Ronnelle, so the sun isn't as prominent. Summer time, they get lots of sun."

The seasons didn't affect how much sun we got back home, not at all. All year we had sun, sun, and more sun. That was why when we got our jackets today, we had to make a big show of it.

The driver said my name was beautiful, but I ignored him and stared out the window some more. I didn't feel bad, and Mum, who usually pinched me when I was rude, didn't feel all that bad either. Anyone who made my Dad clench his fist was no friend of ours. Luckily, the driver knew not to push it.

I noticed there wasn't a lot of trees lining the sidewalks. Maybe one or two in its own dirt square, but other than that, nothing. It made me uncomfortable. There were no signs of bush anywhere.

Where's the bush?

"Dabush?" the driver parroted.

I wanted to roll my eyes. I was speaking English. I looked at Mum, but she was beginning to drift off to sleep with her head slowly falling towards Brendan's.

"Sorry, could you repeat that again for me?"

Where's the bush? How far is the bush?

"Oh, bush? You mean like the forests?"

I nodded, a slow painful nod. He spoke with confusion, yes, but more so fascination. I had a funny feeling that he knew exactly what I was saying, but he just wanted to hear me talk more.

"This is the city, sweetheart. Won't see much forest here." He laughed. Apparently this was amusing to him. I felt sick in my stomach. "We have a few natural parks, though. Very beautiful and green."

Natural parks?

"Sorry, say that again for me? I didn't catch that." I was one-hundred percent sure he had caught it.

But I said it again anyways.

And there was that slug of a smile in the mirror again. I decided from that point that I would not ask anything from him any more. Dramatic, yes, but I made that vow right then and there. I rested my head on Dad's shoulder, seeking some sort of comfort. I wanted him to speak to me in a voice that I could recognize. His voice. Not some voice that pronounced the 'r' in park and a long 'u' in natural.

As if Dad read my mind, he ruffled my hair. "Just keep looking out the window, Ronnie."

I did – and the streets still didn't look gold yet.

Suburbs

Lately I had been a victim to sleep. The maxi ride seemed so long and the buildings in Philly began to look all the same. They followed the same pattern of size and shape and street art. Plus, sleep was the perfect excuse for ignoring the driver when he said something stupid. When I opened my eyes it was because Mum was elbowing me. Used to rude awakenings, I skipped the part where I shoot her a glare and looked straight out the window again.

This was it. This was the suburbs. Our new home. I saw more trees, and there was grass lined up along the sidewalk and in sections wherever the streets ended. I already like it better than the city. The buildings and stores were much farther apart. The signs were bigger, too. There was a Wal-Mart with a parking lot the size of a football field. McDonald's. KFC. A laundromat called Star Laundry. Baked for You.

Kids on bicycles and skateboards and scooters. All different colors. Mummy caught me staring at the group of kids scurrying through the playground. She said they'd be my new friends. I smiled as we turned into, according to the entrance sign, Spring Homes. It sounded pretty. As the maxi drove through the road, twisting and turning along the S-shaped lane, we passed by big houses. Huge houses. Each with their own different color roof and matching window panes.

"They're all two floors with a basement," Mum explained, not directing her voice to anyone in particular. She could have been talking to Brendan for all I knew.

And we're going to live in one of those?

"Sort of," Dad murmured. He looked out his window. I couldn't read his expression.

How long until we get there? I asked. The worst part of any long trip was when you know you're in the area, but you still don't feel like you're even remotely close to the destination. The lady's house could have been any of those houses. While the colors of the exterior changed, they were all as Mum said – two floors. No one answered my question, so I chose a new one to ask: What color is her house?

"Oh gosh, nah. I don't know, Ronnie," Mum said, her eyebrows pinching together. She wasn't all that annoyed. I just kind of snapped her out of her daydream. "Sean?"

Dad snapped out of his daydream too. "The house number is 1307."

There's 1,307 houses in this neighborhood?

"Sure, Ronnie."

I grinned and leaned over Dad's lap to get a better view. He let out a big sigh as protest, but didn't push me off. Good. I couldn't help but feel excited again. Were there even 1,307 houses in a county back home?

"Ronnie, quit shakin' like a Chihuahua! You're making me nervous," Dad said uneasily.

I apologized but my legs didn't stop jittering. My arms felt cold despite the big layer of clothing over me. Out Dad's window I spotted a house with number 1304. The next one was 1306. Then 1308. I was frightened, but as I moved to Mum's window, the odds were on that side. 1307. The very last house on the street, just at the far corner. That meant this house had the most yard space.

The maxi came to a stop and I pushed Mum's door open. Mum sucked her teeth and Dad smacked me on the back.

"Wild child," Mum muttered as she exited the maxi, Brendan held close to her chest. I followed behind while Dad got out on his side. We rounded the back to retrieve our stuff. We only had the two suitcases anyways, so Dad took both and I yelled thanks to the driver. We began heading toward the walkway, a beautiful path of big stones, each one looking like an island on a sea of grass. I hopped on each one.

Dad, aren't you gonna say thank you to the maxi man?

Dad looked at the driver and waved, and the driver nodded and drove off. He looked back at me, holding the suitcases a little higher for a second. "Ronnie, you should know that not all taxis can be called maxis. Only the big ones. The vans. What we just rode in – that was a taxi. Just a taxi."

I nodded slowly.

"Don't sound so annoyed, Sean. She didn't know."

69

"Well I'd like us to sound as less foreign as possible," Dad retorted. "For her sake, at least." He dropped our luggage and knocked on the door.

"Not so hard, Sean. We need to give a good impression." At this point, Mum was exasperated.

We all jumped when the doorknob twisted and screeched. Dad took a step back as the door flung open inwards. In front of us stood a rather unkempt woman. She had frizzy hair tied up in a big bun like Tamika's, except this woman's hair was red and her skin was pale. She had a washed out yellow polo shirt on and a matching skirt with a white apron hanging slack at the hip. Above her breast was a little nametag. Hurt. Was that her first name or her last name? I kept my mouth shut this time before Dad could get on me again. Besides, I was silenced already. She looked exhausted, and her face didn't brighten one bit when she realized who we were.

"Mr. Khan." She looked about twenty-something, but her voice had to be at least forty. Dry. Hollow. Like a coconut after a beach day.

"Ms. Hurt," Dad greeted. He gestured to the three of us. "I'm Sean. This is my family – Kim, Ronnelle, and Brendan."

We all waved, except for Brendan, who just blinked.

"Lovely." The word seemed irrelevant to her expression. "I'll show you where you'll be staying."

She took a step back with the door in her hand and we moved towards her.

"Wait. Go around to the backdoor. Right around there, can't miss it. I'll let you in." She disappeared and we were left with a door in our face.

I looked up at Dad to try and read his expression. Why couldn't we come inside this way? Mum was the first to move on from the moment and march across the grass on the side of the house. The lawn sloped downward. We rounded the corner. The side of her house was perfect for growing vegetables in a neat row. Mum was thinking the same thing. She stared as well.

We reached the back door in a matter of seconds. It looked nothing like the front door. The front door was wooden and dark, definitely neat and smoothed over. The back door was white and when I tapped my finger against it, it sounded weak. If there was a storm the door would be the first to get shot into the sky. Dad placed his hand on my shoulder. I didn't know if it was for comfort or if it was to push me back.

The door opened. This time the knob didn't make a screechy sound. It clicked a few times and there was a grunting noise as well, but that was probably the woman. She eyed the four of us as if she were making a quick headcount, and then let us in. We funneled into the house as she told us to move faster. The door shut.

We were in her basement, and her basement was our new home.

The Hurt Basement

Dad called it the Hurt basement, pouting his face at the word "hurt" to imply that that was how the basement felt. It always made me laugh. Ignoring the fact that we were supposed to live in a basement, this new home was an upgrade. There were two beds, one for Mum and Dad, and one for me (Dad said he'd buy a crib for Brendan when the time comes). Beside the smaller bed was the door to a little bathroom. The bathroom was complete with a black toilet, white crusty sink, and a single shower with no door. On the opposite wall of my parents' bed was a fridge and a separate freezer that opened like a cooler. Both were empty. Beside the fridge, in the very corner of the basement, was the staircase leading up.

Now, "up" was where Ms. Hurt lived. "Up" was basically the rest of the house, the part of the house we weren't allowed to go in, or even see. In fact, at the top of those stairs was a door. Ms. Hurt always kept it locked. The day we moved in, as she was leaving to go up the stairs, she told us "under no circumstance" were we allowed to go up there. When she said that, Mum, Dad, and I all looked at one another. Mum's lips quivered. Dad's frown tightened but he called out his fifth thank you. I, on the other hand, giggled.

Under no circumstance.

It wasn't like we could get up there anyways. She kept that door locked like she had visitors and we were the naughty dogs that had to be kept away. I didn't mind. The basement was great, much comfier than the step-house. Colder, but comfier. We still only had one closet, but at least the beds didn't take up the majority of the floor space. I could run in a circle and not bump into anything.

We settled in pretty quickly considering we only had our two suitcases to unpack. All of our clothes fit comfortably in the closet by the back door. Dad found an empty cardboard box in the closet and used it to put some of Brendan's baby stuff.

In the basement, I dealt with what little we had. I liked to play house. While Dad made calls and found himself occupied with the papers, and Mum took care of Brendan and slept, I would pretend the bare fridge was stocked with food and the lid of the freezer was my sink and stove. As I chopped the air the way Mum did when she cut pork for stew, I gazed at the chalky grey wall and pretended it was my camera. For just a moment, I was a famous chef and had an audience of people of all color.

Mum caught me once and said she promised we'd make grocery trips. She was partially correct. *We* didn't make the grocery trip – Dad did. He wobbled in with a couple plastic bags. I emptied all of them out on our beds. A box of cornflakes. A big holy bag of red grapes. A bag of potato bread. A gallon of milk.

That's a lot of milk.

"They sell them smaller, but you get more for less money if you buy the gallon," Dad explained, probably not to me.

Mum put the grapes and milk in the fridge, and the cereal and bread on top of it. "There's no milk man?"

Dad shrugged.

I wasn't a dumb kid. With parents like mine, and the dozens of books I'd read, I learned to figure things out on my own when I could. For instance, Dad didn't like all of us leaving to head outside at the same time because it would be "too obvious." I didn't know *why* that was a problem, but I knew Ms. Hurt didn't want people to know we were bunking in the basement.

Mum let me play outside when I heard something hitting the side of the basement. It had to be a ball. I ducked out the back and ran towards the kids across the street. There was a large square of grass between houses 1308 and 1310. That was where the kids went out to play a lot. The ones outside on this particular day were Rafael and Kyle. Rafael was short for a ten-year-old, with black spiky hair and long eyelashes that brushed against his glasses every time he blinked. Kyle was a chubby nine-year-old with long brown hair that needed to be cut. I couldn't see his eyes all that much. They were kicking a football back and forth, and occasionally Kyle would miss and the white ball would smack against a car. Each time, the boys would run behind a bush and giggle for a few seconds. Then they'd come out, retrieve the ball, and start over. Getting a grasp of this routine, I ran to the field and blocked a pass that was headed for Rafael.

"Aw, come on!" Kyle whined. He kicked the grass.

"You're fast!" Rafael cheered.

I grinned and finished the pass to Rafael.

This was actually the first time I ever approached them. Before I had only watched from Ms. Hurt's lawn. Anytime they'd turn their head in my direction, I'd pretend to be fascinated by the worms swirling through the dirt.

Rafael, do you play for a team?

Rafael looked at me and nodded his head. "Yeah. My dad is the coach."

You too, Kyle?

"Yeah. Same team as Raffy." Kyle was still not looking at me.

Neither boy asked how I knew their names. After their football time, their mums would usually yell their name from the doorstep, probably calling them in for dinner. That was how I learned them.

Pass me the football.

I took a few steps away, making a triangle amongst the three of us.

"This isn't a football, stupid," Kyle said. "It's a soccer ball."

Rafael juggled the ball on his knees, only lasting two taps before the ball hit the ground again. "My uncles call it football. It's okay." He passed it to me.

I stopped the ball with the inside of my foot like Uncle Johnny taught me. Rafael giggled and waved me over, urging me to pass the ball back to him. Kyle, on the other hand, got angry again, and sat himself down on the grass.

"Kyle, what's wrong?" Rafael asked. He got the ball from me and kicked it in Kyle's direction. It was meant to be a light pass, but it seemed more like a goal shot, and it hit Kyle right on the head.

As expected, Kyle screamed and flung his hands to his head. I was more than positive it didn't hurt that much, but I needed to make friends, so I went up to Kyle and patted him on the shoulder. The gesture didn't work. He screamed even louder than I thought was possible and in seconds the sound of his mother's shrill voice rang from house 1310.

Your mum is calling you.

Kyle kept crying.

Kyle, your mum is calling you!

Rafael and I both reached our hand out to help Kyle to his feet, but Kyle only took Rafael's hand, so as he stood, he lost balance and fell back down. He was a little heavy after all. I stuck my hand out again and Kyle finally accepted it. He stood and made a run for his house.

"Kyle, why are you being a baby?" Rafael called after his friend.

"I'm not the baby. *She's* the baby!" Kyle yelled back, stopping in his tracks to make a big show of pointing his sausage finger at me. "She wants all the attention!"

Rafael looked back at me, and I shrugged. What was I supposed to say? When we tried to look at Kyle again, the boy was already in his house, probably in his mum's lap.

Rafael picked up his football and pointed to house 1308. "I'm gonna go home, too."

And he left. Apparently that was his way of saying good-bye. At that point, I thought there was still a chance I could make friends. Everyone talked real slow here, but I would learn to tolerate it. I didn't bother staying outside any longer. I went around Ms. Hurt's house to the backdoor. Knocked five times. Mum let me in.

So this first week in the Hurt basement was something. Playing house. Trying to make friends. Failing. Eating cereal and bread and grapes. We used the bathroom sink water when we got thirsty, but by the middle of the week Dad said he may just buy us packages of bottled water instead. We never really did that before, so Mum told me it was probably because Dad doesn't trust the water here. I agreed. It did taste a little different. Almost like it was *too* clean.

My biggest issue was night time. Dad bought a wall clock and a car seat from some place he and Mum referred to as G.W. The car seat was put in the corner directly next to their bed, and adjacent from mine. Brendan's crib. Dad claimed it was new, but I saw the tear in the cloth, as if the buckles that were supposed to secure the baby were ripped out by a tiger. It was soft, though. I gave him that.

At night, Mum would put Brendan in the car seat along with a thick blanket. She'd say something silly, like "you're going to have great posture at such a young age, Brendan." She'd climb in bed with Dad, who wasn't always there on time but he always showed up in the end (I didn't even attempt to sleep until he got home), and they'd whisper and whisper until Mum fell asleep first. I couldn't sleep through their whispers. I was always a sensitive sleeper. Everything had to be perfect and uniform before I could even lay still. Once the whispers went away and Mum's unladylike snores rang through the room, I'd shut my eyes tight and hug my pillow. I didn't ever use it for my head anymore. I needed something to hold. No one was on the bed with me.

I felt kind of like Grandma.

I hardly got any sleep during the night. Sometimes I'd hear my screaming goat and feel a bit better. Or sometimes I pretended there was a window near the bed and I'd imagine Butch sleeping just outside of it, breathing heavily. Wednesday, I tried to sneak Brendan into my bed, but Dad caught me. I didn't know how – I was quiet compared to Mum's motor mouth – but he did, and he sent me back to bed.

But by Friday I realized something. Dad wasn't sleeping either. I had trouble keeping my eyes closed that night, and I was ready to steal Brendan again. I didn't want Dad to catch me, so I slithered off my bed and tiptoed to his first to check if his eyes were closed.

And they weren't.

"Ronnie."

Daddy?

Dad scooted over, closer to the edge of the bed, and lowered the blanket so I could slip between him and Mum. I didn't ask him why he was up.

"I haven't slept since we got here."

Me too.

I lied, but my eyes sure did feel like they hadn't slept for a week. I began to close them, but they shot open again when I felt the bed shake. Dad had gotten up and walked over to Brendan. He picked him up and walked back to the bed, setting Brendan behind me, near Mum's head. He got back in bed and we stared at each other.

"We'll get good sleep tonight."

I smiled, even though he probably couldn't see it very clearly in the dark. I was slowly drifting off to sleep with the feel of his big hand on my back. I imagined Lenny's happy bleat, and Butch's chubby breaths, and the scratchy male voice through the wall. I imagined all of these things that made me feel safe: my entire family on the bed, all of us squished together by choice.

It feels like home again.

True Journalism

Because Ms. Hurt kept the door upstairs locked, I didn't see her all that often. It was unfortunate for me considering I had set a goal hoping to touch her hair one day. I had never physically seen someone with red hair, let alone red hair with a texture similar to Tamika's. I did manage to sneak a few glances of her outside. Sometimes she'd come home from work and slam the door really, really loud. I figured out from this routine that she worked until four, just like Dad had mentioned at the motel. I tried to be outside when she came home. I sat at the edge of the curb, not too close to her house, but close enough to get the perfect view of her hair poofed out in every direction. One time she spotted me and we gazed at each other for a few seconds as she froze by her front door. She was the first to look away, turning her head back to the house after twisting her lip.

I was dying to know more about her. After all, she was doing my entire family a favor. I didn't know how much money our own place would cost, but I knew it was less than what she was charging Dad. I also knew that not many people rented out their basement. At least, that was what Mum whispered to Dad one night before he shushed her.

Apparently I had one week left to settle in before Mum and Dad would make me attend school. While Mum stayed home with Brendan, Dad said he'd buy me some more clothes.

Clothes for what?

"Clothes for school," Dad answered.

"G.W?" Mum asked.

"G.W," Dad answered.

I knew how to spell. I could spell very well because I could read very well, but the letters G and W alone didn't make any word I could think of. When I asked what G.W. was, both Mum and Dad said pretty blatantly that it was just a store. Mum went back to cuddling Brendan. Dad left. I looked at the wall clock. It was four o'clock. Ms. Hurt was going to be home soon. I had to start acting on my goal.

After letting Mum know I wanted to go outside, I ran out to the curb and waited and waited for Ms. Hurt to come walking down the sidewalk past house 1303 and 1305. She walked heavily on her heels, her toes barely having time to hit the ground before being thrown in front of her again. Her hair had its usual afro-nature.

Across the road, Rafael and Kyle were kicking the football again. I waved but neither boy returned it. Their eyes were focused on Ms. Hurt. They looked scared. Kyle's fear was no surprise, but Rafael looked a bit baffled as well. Therefore, before Ms. Hurt could even step on her lawn, I disappeared through the back of the house and sat myself next to Mum. That night, Dad brought back four new T-shirts and two pairs of pants. I asked where my uniform was. He said I didn't need a uniform for this school. Then he said we'd all go shoe shopping some other day. G.W. didn't have adequate shoes.

The next day, which was a Monday, I figured I'd try again. Mum stayed home. Dad went out to work. I didn't know what his job was but I knew it was something decent because the day he shared the good news, he didn't have his black socks on. Any time Dad didn't have his socks on, something great was happening. Again, Mum let me outside at four o'clock.

Rafael and Kyle weren't outside this time. Maybe they were in trouble. I took their absence as encouragement to talk to Ms. Hurt. The boys wouldn't be there to intimidate me.

As expected, Ms. Hurt stomped her way towards the house, her apron lifting in the air at each angry step.

How was work today, Ms. Hurt?

Ms. Hurt paused on one of the stones leading to her front door. Like a scene from a horror movie, she turned her head towards me and I felt myself shrink into the curb.

"Really? You too?"

I didn't know what she was talking about. Did she think I was someone else? That couldn't be right. No one looked like me here. At least, that's what I assumed.

"Not today, kid." She was already by the front door by this time. Within seconds, she was inside, and I was the size of an ant.

Maybe tomorrow.

And tomorrow came. Dad left for work. Mum stayed home, but this time her attention was divided between Brendan and a bunch of papers she refused to let me see every time I tried to look over her shoulder. She shooed me outside.

The boys were nowhere to be seen. They must have really got in trouble. I sat on my usual spot, but as soon as Ms. Hurt passed me, I shot to my feet. It must have alarmed her because she tripped when she reached her lawn.

"How do you get home from school earlier than the other kids?" She didn't sound curious. Just irritated.

But I was pleased she initiated a conversation. And I was shocked to find she didn't pronounce her H's. Or, I guess, *couldn't*. I doubt it was a choice.

I'm not in school yet.

"Whaddya mean? You're ten, aren't you?"

I nodded. I start next week.

"Geez, I don't even remember – what is that? Middle school or elementary?"

What?

"What school?"

Oh. Primary school.

"Primary school," Ms. Hurt murmured. She sighed and rubbed her thumbs again the end of her pale yellow skirt stained with something orange. "Over here, it's called elementary school, okay, kid?" She was by the front door. "I'm doing you a favor, trust me. Kids like it when you can't speak right."

And she was gone. She was gone, but I felt one step closer to touching her hair.

On Wednesday I was feeling lucky. The day before, I managed somewhat of a conversation with Ms. Hurt, so today I felt like I was really

STREETS OF MELTED GOLD

getting somewhere. The routine went on as planned. Mum home. Dad work. I got permission to go outside. Rafael and Kyle were nowhere to be seen, but judging from what Ms. Hurt said the day before, they just weren't home from school yet.

I waited at the curb, but this time I didn't even bother to sit. I was excited. I hopped up and down, waiting and keeping myself entertained until the dot approaching me shifted into a sleepy woman. Sleepy, but happy. She looked happy. Her hair was tied up in a bun and not spilling out. It looked neat. She looked happy and neat.

I waved. Ms. Hurt!

"Ronnelle," she replied.

My hand froze in the air. She had remembered my name.

"Is this how the kids play back in your country? Stalking adults? Are you their youngest reporter?"

I laughed. I didn't know she had a sense of humor.

She reached the lawn but didn't make a move toward her house. The corner of her mouth quirked upward. "Easy crowd."

I shrugged.

I like laughing, Ms. Hurt.

"That's nice, kid." Ms. Hurt untied the stained apron from her waist and folded it up in her hands. "But I was talking about the crowd at work today."

Where do you work?

"Where do you think?" She gestured toward her uniform.

I know it's a restaurant but what restaurant?

"Whitman's."

Who?

She sighed. "That's just the name."

I must have started to bore her because she began moving toward her front door again.

Is work usually awful?

She stopped. "Awful," she repeated.

But today was nice?

Ms. Hurt turned to me. "Yeah. Yeah it was nice. Big birthday party. Bunch of happy drunk fat men."

Why was today nice and all the other days awful?

Her hands slid into the pocket that had been hidden behind the apron. She pulled out a bunch of folded cash. It was all green.

That's a lot of fives!

"These aren't just fives, kid. I've got four twenties, three tens, a five, and two ones."

But there's only green.

"Over here, that's the only color dollars come in."

I stared at the money. That was something I did not know.

"That's another thing you need to remember when you start school next week."

After a pause, I spoke again. Thanks.

I looked down to the curb. It occurred to me that the kids I'd meet at school, if they were anything like Kyle, would be very different from me. I felt Ms. Hurt's eyes on me, but eventually she turned around and headed for her front door again. I watched her.

"Don't call me Hurt anymore, alright? Makes me feel old. Call me Jessica." She kept her eyes focused on the doorknob.

I felt a smile sneaking up on my face, but I wanted to stay cool.

Call me Ronnie.

And we both went inside our separate homes.

Thursday arrived. Everything was the same. Instead of the curb, I stood on the lawn. Ms. Hurt walked straight up to me since she really had no choice. Her hair was in an afro-y mess. There were lines across her forehead. She was upset. Messy and upset.

Work was awful.

It was a strange moment. We had both said that statement at the exact time, as if we were one voice alone.

Ms. Hurt was on the sidewalk. I was standing on one of the flat stones on her yard.

Did you make money?

"I don't make money. I make tips. That's all I make. But today? Today I made fifteen dollars."

You only get tips?

"I get paid what, three-something an hour. The rest has to be in tips. When I don't make much tip, I'm screwed. So right now? I'm screwed." Ms. Hurt walked over to the curb where I usually had settled and she fell onto her bottom. Her shoulders slumped and she rested her elbows on her knees. "I got student loans to pay off. Thousands of dollars spent to take journalism, and here I am."

I walked over to her. I was terrified to sit down beside her with the way Kyle and Rafael had stared in fear the previous Sunday.

But I found myself sitting down next to her anyway.

You walk to work every day?

She nodded. "Once you hit the community entrance, you take a left and boom you're there. Can't miss the big obnoxious burger with sunglasses sticking out of the top of the building."

I stayed quiet, trying to think of something else to say. Something that wouldn't encourage her to regret speaking to me.

"The restaurant's got a bar, but we're so desperate for customers, we only get the weird ones. I mean, the only people who'd spend their afternoon at a bar on a work day are the weirdos. Lucky me." She flicked a crumb off of her thigh.

Why don't you quit?

I remembered Mum had quit this one job she had before the nail salon. She had been an expediter at a little Indian cuisine place. She hated it. The building was too hot and the boss was lost in tabanca for her. Apparently she and he had a thing in secondary school ages ago. Once Dad found out he said either she could quit or all hell would break loose at "Gupta's." Gupta's wasn't even the name of the place.

"'Cause I'm stuck like some of the stains on my apron." She huffed, and I could've sworn it was the start of a chuckle, but the way she muttered and stood to her feet made me think otherwise.

I wish my family was more stuck.

I can't remember if I even said that out loud or not, but right afterwards, Ms. Hurt trudged toward her front door again.

I thought maybe I had to give her a break and stop bugging her. I stood and started to walk around the side of the house. Before I was completely out of her sight, she poked her head around the corner and looked at me – not necessarily my eyes, but my hair.

"Is it too cold in there? The heat doesn't reach, but I could lower the AC."

I copied her gaze and looked at her red hair.

Is it too cold for you upstairs?

"No. I'm perfectly fine."

Then we're perfectly fine.

And we went inside our separate homes.

Friday didn't begin as I had hoped. Sure, Dad had gone and Mum let me leave. I stood on the front lawn and waited. Waited some more. It seemed longer than the other days, so I ran back into the basement and checked the wall clock for the time. It was a quarter to five. Mum was napping on the bed, so I didn't have to explain why I poked my head back in the house. I sat myself on the curb now, my face buried in my hands. It was getting chilly again. It was like Mum said. Fall was here. I hadn't worn my new jacket all week besides our first day in Philly because the weather had been better since then. But now it was getting cold again. I tucked my hands in the sleeves of my shirt and squinted down the street.

And I think I fell asleep. My eyes had closed, and when they opened, Kyle and Rafael were across the street, but they weren't playing yet. They had book bags on their backs and were headed to their houses. Faces sweaty, breathing heavy. Do they play somewhere else during the weekdays? They didn't take notice of me, and I was grateful for that.

Once they were out of sight I stood to my feet. I thought maybe something was wrong. Ms. Hurt's job was awful. I tightened the laces on my sneakers and bolted down the street, goosebumps and all. I wanted my jacket, and I wanted it badly, but I couldn't risk running into Mum and being questioned.

Ms. Hurt had told me exactly where Whitman's was. *Take a left and boom you're there.* Easy. Plus all I had to look for was a burger with shades. The trip itself was terribly easy. The sidewalks here were so smooth and even, different from the questionable sidewalks I used to take to get to the step-house from school. There weren't much hills either. Everything was just, well, flat. As a kid who climbed trees and hopped from bush to bush, this was a piece of cake.

I reached the entrance sign to Spring Homes in no time. From there, I took a left. There was a moderate amount of cars on the road because it was around five o'clock and I was smart enough to know that was when work began to end for the day.

Usually when I walked through my own neighborhood, I at least spotted one person I knew and would holler their name and say hello, but I couldn't do that here. I hoped, though, that one day I could do that again. But until then, everyone I passed just sped by as if I didn't exist. That was OK. If people were anything like our taxi, not maxi, driver, I didn't want to speak to them anyways.

Thankfully the lonely walk was over and I found the building. It was a perfectly cube-shaped diner. On top was of course the burger, a cartoony fat figure with a cheesy smile and toothpick legs. The parking lot looked like it could fit about ten cars. I would have counted but the paint on the lot was barely visible to mark the spaces. I tugged open the heavy entrance door and made my way inside.

It wasn't all that pretty. No wonder they didn't bother to invest in a bigger lot. Who would come to this place? There were five black booths against the window and three free standing tables. The booth seats didn't look very soft, and the only customer in the dining area was in the very corner booth by himself. All he needed was a "Do Not Disturb" sign.

Looking to the left now, that was where the bar was located. A long wooden counter with a bunch of glasses and bottles lining the back wall. There were some bar stools sprinkled about. A karaoke machine in the corner. That side was a little busier – there were more than six people with drinks in their hands, although they all looked like they were together.

Well, they sure acted like they were together. They were all loud and hysterical as they looped arms around one another and joked about each others' kids. I searched around for Ms. Hurt. She wasn't anywhere that I could see, so I approached the only visible staff member – the bartender.

He was middle-aged, probably in his early fifties, and he was white. His hair was completely gray, but full. Reached his ears. Despite the age, he had the face of a baby. Clean shaven with wide eyes. I could've sworn the left one was twitching. If I had to stay and wait for those clients to leave, mine would end up twitching too.

Hello.

Dressed in a black shirt with a nametag that read Steve, he peered over the counter at me. "Hi." It sounded more like a question.

I'm looking for Ms. Hurt.

He raised a thin eyebrow. "What's she to you, little lady?"

I glanced around the diner. She's my friend.

"Jessica hanging with a kid? That's new."

He didn't believe me.

"Listen, kid, if you're here to bother Ms. Hurt, scram. She's had a rough day and frankly I'm sick of your generation coming in here and bothering her. She's got enough in her neighborhood. Don't bring it to her workplace, too." He motioned his hand as if to say *shoo*.

By his hand I noticed a little tip glass that looked like it had previously been a jar of jam. I dug through my pocket and took out a one. I always kept a little bit of change on me because it made me feel like an adult. I flattened it on the counter and looked up at Mr. Steve as I did so.

I'm her friend.

"What's this?" He chuckled. "A bribe?"

No, it's a tip.

"For who? Where's your parents?"

It's for Ms. Hurt. When she doesn't make much tips, she's *screwed*.

He stared at me. "This dollar is red."

I know, but it adds up, doesn't it? If she gets a lot of ones, it'll add up and she can-

"Ronnie?"

Ms. Hurt was standing in front of the kitchen door with a plate of fries and a bottle of ketchup in her hand. With her uniform and apron and plate, she really did look like a waitress. Especially with her hair in a bun. It was pretty messy today, that bun. Strands were popping out in every direction. Her head looked like the sun, rays and all. I smiled at her.

Ms. Hurt!

Ms. Hurt didn't look very happy. She briskly headed to the corner booth with the lonely man and set his food in front of him. Then she headed straight for me. Her brown eyes looked tired as she looked between me and the bartender. Finally they settled.

"Did she ask you anything, Andrew? What the hell are you doing here? Are you alone?"

I nodded. You were taking forever to come home.

"So you just up and left the house? I'm a grown woman, Ronnie. You don't need to check up on me at work."

Mr. Steve coughed. He opened his mouth like he was going to chime in but a customer called out for a *Summer Ale*. He turned away to get it.

I was worried, Ms. Hurt.

"What did I say about calling me that?"

Jessica.

"And where are your parents?"

Mummy is home and Dad is working.

"Do they know you're here?"

I shook my head.

Her hand found her forehead. "Go home, kid. Please."

My bottom lip trembled. She was kicking me out. Did she not want me here at all?

"Go home. This is no place for a kid without any parents around. Go home."

Okay. We can walk home together.

"No. We can't. I'm still here today 'cause I'm working a *double*, Ronnie. I won't be home until ten when the kitchen closes."

Part of me was relieved to find that she wasn't purposely avoiding me. The other part was unsatisfied.

"Go. Home."

Fine. I picked up the dollar from the counter and stuffed it in the empty tip jar. As I began to turn around, Ms. Hurt snatched the same dollar from the tip jar and smacked it against my arm.

"Seriously, kid, you've got to leave me alone. For your sake, leave me alone. I don't need this from you."

I can't.

"Go home, Ronnie. Please."

I nodded. I took my dollar and went for the same doors I had entered through. Before I even laid a finger on the door, I glanced back and saw Mr. Steve and Ms. Hurt whispering, both matching with their pinched eyebrows and the rapid movement of their mouths. I ran to the lonely man in the corner and placed my dollar on his booth.

Give her this tip, please.

And I left Whitman's with one single thought in my head: I would never leave Ms. Hurt alone.

New Shoes

I hadn't seen Ms. Hurt since the restaurant incident, which was alright with me. She needed to cool down. Plus I was busy with my parents the following Saturday anyways. Dad got a *taxi* and we took a family trip to a shoe store. I was pleased that the driver was a different man. This one had chocolate skin and a big sloppy grin on his face. He didn't say anything – he just smiled and drove. I liked him.

Just like before, I was told to sit in the middle. I didn't mind so much this time since yesterday's walk got me acquainted more with what there was to see. Plus the drive to Spring Homes showed me everything I needed to see: stores and parking lots and flat sidewalks and strips of grass. Some bus stops scattered throughout the street.

The shoe store wasn't very far. Honestly, we could have walked and got there within thirty minutes, but Dad said he didn't want anyone to have to hold Brendan for that long. The weather was also getting chillier by the day.

The building was short with a grey exterior and the name of the shoe store was spelled in orange and yellow.

Pay Less Shoe Store.

"Shoe *source*. It says source."

That's weird.

We exited the taxi and Dad paid him off with a bunch of green dollars, telling him to wait. When we entered the store, a lady behind the counter waved and said there were a bunch of "bogo" sales that we should "take advantage of" today.

Bogo?

Mum kissed Brendan on the forehead. "Buy one, get one..." She squinted at the sign above the eager worker's head. "Fifty percent off." She elbowed Dad. "Wow, Sean. We came on a good day."

We walked through the store, scanning the aisles. Dad said we all could get anything we need within reason. He disappeared in the men's aisle with Brendan while I stayed with Mum in the size four section. I picked out a pair of red sneakers and swung them in front of her by the laces.

Nice, ent?

"Yes, but look." She pointed at the white sneakers I was already wearing. "You don't need new ones. You've got those. Here, get some boots."

Boots?

I never liked boots. They were harder to run in. I followed Mum further down the aisle and she picked up black rubber boots that were lined with some sort of cloth on the inside for comfort.

"Good price. Okay, we got your shoes. I think I'll get some sneakers for myself."

Mum went in the size nine section and in an instant she found a pair of black sneakers. She handed me the boxes and told me to wait up by the cashier if no one was in line. So I did as she said and tossed the boxes on the counter.

I'm waiting on my mum.

The lady smiled really big at me. So big her eyes looked closed. "Don't you have the cutest accent?"

Thank you, I like yours too.

She laughed and flung her head back. I was scared. Luckily Mum, Dad, and Brendan joined us with another two boxes. Brendan was placed in my arms as Mum and Dad handled the purchases. The lady kept staring at Mum's hair, even as she bagged the boxes.

"Your hair is gorgeous, I've got to say. How do you get the curls to stay so stretched? It's beautiful!"

Mum took the bags from the counter. "Ah, thank you. I just wash and go."

"Beautiful! Just beautiful! My daughter would kill to have hair-"

We began walking away as politely as possible, but the woman went on and on that by the time half of us were out the door, she was still babbling. I doubt she even noticed we left. We rode the taxi home and put our shoes under our beds.

That day, Dad went out again and brought home a large pizza for us to share. It was great, a change from the quick foods we bought and stored all week. The pizza had pineapple and ham and peppers. As we ate on the floor and Brendan lay comfortably on my bed, Mum brought up how much she wanted to put some pepper sauce on her slice. She and Dad loved things spicy. Any chance they got, Mum would put half a spoon of hot sauce or pepper sauce on her food. But for now, they just had to deal with the mild taste.

We laughed and ate and talked. Mum brought up how I kept going outside to play and asked if I made any friends.

Not really.

"What? You've been playing by yourself? Kids don't play outside around here?" Mum asked. She wouldn't know. She had been bottled up in the basement for a while now.

Dad shook his head. "Nah. The kids play. I've seen them at the playground near the entrance."

I shrugged.

"Met anyone you like, at least?"

I nodded.

"Who?"

They live across the street and like to play foot – ah, soccer. They like soccer. I think they're my age.

"Maybe you'll meet them at school on Monday," Mum said.

Then things suddenly turned serious. Dad put his pizza slice down.

"Ronnie, you listen to me and your mum, okay?"

Okay?

"If anybody, and I mean *anybody*, including your teacher, asks you where you're from, you don't tell them anything. You hear me?"

I nodded slowly.

"Well, gosh, Sean. What's she supposed to say, then?"

"We already discussed this. Just tell them you're from out of town. That's all they need to know. Americans are real nosey."

"Tell her about the whole living situation, too, Sean."

"Right. Ronnie, you listening?"

I nodded.

"If anyone asks where you live, just tell them we're in-laws of Ms. Hurt and we wanted to move here but needed a place to stay before we could settle."

"Shucks."

"What, Kim?"

"That's a mouthful. Give her something simple."

"Just tell them Ms. Hurt is your God-mother."

"Aunt would be much simpler."

"The woman is an only child. You think she bought this house on her own? She was on her grandmother's will, Kim. God-mother could mean anything. Aunt is too specific and too controversial."

My mind felt dizzy.

"Got it, child?"

Yes.

"Good girl. Go to bed, nah. Your eyes are closing on us." Dad moved Brendan from my bed to his. "Don't forget what we said."

"She won't, Sean. I know you're gonna say it again tomorrow night."

The Jingle

I was a weird kid. Going to a new country, a new home, to a new school – I was taking it pretty well. At first, that is. For instance, the very last day before school started for me, which was a Sunday, school wasn't on my mind at all. I had new clothes and new shoes. Dad got me a transparent plastic backpack and two folders. He gave me two pencils and warned me not to lose them. I kept my school things in the corner, out of mind's way.

What was on my mind was this chant some kids made up on the playground. Seeing that it was Sunday and not as chilly as the past couple days, I went outside to walk about. Instead of lingering on the lawn, I wanted to try out the playground up by the entrance where apparently the other kids liked to play.

The playground was partially hidden by the trees, meaning cars on the main road couldn't peek in unless they turned into the community. It was nice and secluded. A swing set, a slide, monkey bars, and a dome-shaped jungle gym. The kids present were crowding the swing set and slide, but I liked climbing things better anyway. I scaled to the top of the jungle gym and sat myself at the center.

There were children of all colors and ages and heights. It felt a little weird, but I liked the diversity. There were more white kids than any of the others, but there were still others. As I swung my legs back and forth, I heard a familiar scream from behind me.

Kyle? I looked back and there he was, standing at the bottom of the jungle gym with his fists clenched and trembling. Next to him was short Rafael, arms crossed. They weren't looking at me, though. They were busy looking at the itty bitty scrape on Kyle's arm. I rolled my eyes and hopped off the bars. It was pretty high up, so as I fell I thought of how I jumped from the mango tree with Adam and had to tuck and roll at the bottom.

Hi, guys.

Kyle didn't say anything. He just turned away while pouting at the scrape, which was already beginning to fade.

93

"Hi," Rafael said. He hardly paid any attention to Kyle's cut. "You talk to the Hurt lady?"

I nodded.

"Why would you do that? She'll hurt you!"

I tilted my head to the side. Hurt me?

"Haven't you heard the song?"

I shook my head and Rafael took me by the arm, yelling to the kids on the swings that I never heard the song. They stopped their swinging and all eyes were set on me.

Don't end up like poor young Burt,

Never talk to Lady Hurt.

I wanted to laugh. They looked so serious, and the song was more like a creepy, poorly written chant than anything else.

Who's Burt?

"Burt was a kid who tried to talk to Ms. Hurt. The next day, him and his family disappeared." A little girl wearing a plaid dress with puffy pigtails stared at me. "She's crazy!"

"Yeah!"

"Her name is *Hurt.*"

"Have you seen her hair?"

"She's got witch hair!"

I looked between all the faces and wanted to run away. The Burt story must have been a lie. Some made up story. Or maybe it was true, but they got it all wrong. Maybe Burt's family suddenly decided to move away? I mean, we did, after all. And how convenient was it that his name rhymed with hers? If this was how the kids would be at school, my excitement was headed downhill already. It wasn't that high to begin with.

"The last new girl didn't believe us either," Rafael pointed out. "Guys, we gotta show her!"

Seconds after that exclamation I found myself engulfed in a crowd of children fleeing the playground and heading down the road. I kept running because if I were to go in any other direction I'd get pushed back in the middle. I knew exactly where we were headed: Ms. Hurt's house.

We stopped at the tip of the lawn and three kids removed themselves from the mob. Two boys and a girl, all looking like standard five kids, maybe standard six because the girl was a little grown. I watched as the three of them walked to the front door. I had never dared to walk up to that door since our arrival. The girl lifted her fist up and the other boys did the same. On their own count, they pounded their hands against it three times.

"You need to go to church!" one boy yelled toward the house.

The other boy laughed and clapped his hands in sick delight. "You can't touch us while we're outside!"

The kids around me were giggling away, so focused on the clowns by the door that they didn't see that Ms. Hurt was positioned by her window on the second floor. The curtains were drawn, but I saw her fingers gripping the middle, like she was considering looking out.

"Give Burt back!"

"He's probably locked in the basement!"

Something came over me. My feet were moving before my brain could respond and I found myself smashing my foot against one of the door-knockers' stomach.

"The new girl kicked her!"

The group of kids spilled onto the sidewalk to the lawn. My hair was pulled. My shoulders were punched. Over the other kids' voices I could hear Rafael yelling stop to the two boys who were hitting me. I didn't care. I screamed and dived for one of the boy's ankles, causing him to slam to the grass. The other boy, shocked that his friend was now lying on the ground instead of pulling at my braid, froze. Easy enough. I pulled him by the wrist and then pushed him to the ground, too.

This wasn't my first fight. I had one or two back home, way before the step-house. I wasn't an angry kid, I promise. I had legitimate reasons for the brawls – one because a kid pushed me off the swings to get her turn, and the other because my friend was being teased for being "so dark she was purple." I had legitimate reasons.

And now I was fighting to knock some sense into the delusional children I sadly had to call my neighbors. I was about to clout the older girl when she held her hand up to my face and narrowed her eyes.

"Whose side are you on?"

What sides? There's no sides!

"Hurt is evil! She'll *hurt* you."

Hurt is just her last name! You can't choose your last name.

"Then what's her first name?"

I hesitated. I knew it was Jessica, of course I knew, but I wanted to keep that to myself. For us all to know what Ms. Hurt's first name was meant that I was at the same level as the others. I didn't want to be at their level. I was past them.

Well, it's not Hurt!

"She needs to be put in jail!"

I eyed the little stub of a child that made that comment. She looked hardly five. That was enough to make me snap. Well, snap a second time.

Everybody off my lawn!

Everyone looked at my finger pointing toward the street. They slowly began to disperse, including Kyle who looked happy to leave. A few lingered.

I said get off!

"This is not your lawn, liar."

Yes it is! Get off! Get off!

A couple kids laughed.

"You sound funny."

I stalked closer to them and they ran off the lawn. Then I looked back at Rafael, the older girl, and the two boys on the ground.

"Burt is in the basement."

"This can't be your lawn. Burt's trapped inside."

Burt's not trapped inside! I am!

I hadn't meant it like that, although thinking about it now, I was telling the truth. We did feel cooped up inside. Luckily the others were quiet, so I was able to explain myself without them interrupting me.

Ms. Hurt is my God-mother. My family needs a place to stay before we get a house like you guys. Houses are expensive.

"Where are you from?"

I looked at the front door. Don't tell anyone where you come from until you know it's OK. It was definitely not OK yet.

Out of town, I finally answered.

"I don't believe you." The older girl helped get the other boys to their feet and the three of them began to walk off.

I didn't mind. I just wanted them to get off my lawn. Rafael looked at them, and then at me.

"I have to go eat lunch."

I waved and he ran off. My eyes immediately trailed to the second floor window again. Ms. Hurt was still there. I wanted to wave at her too, but I thought that may be pushing it too far. So I pulled the woogie from my disheveled braid and let my hair fall over my shoulders. My head was sore from the pulling it had experienced, but I knew I felt better than the boys did.

Ms. Hurt pulled the curtains open and we gazed at each other for a while. Then she disappeared. The window opened and out dropped a new woogie for my hair. She must have thought mine had broken. I searched the grass and found it. I might as well have put it on out of gratitude, so I did. It was a bright green color and held my hair in a tight ponytail. We made eye contact again as she shut the window. Then she disappeared for good.

I found myself skipping as I rounded the house to the backdoor, forgetting the Hurt song altogether. I was just happy I got to see her. Or rather, I was happy she let me.

Broken Glass

Ms. Hurt had been right. Kids did like it when they found something wrong with you. They ate it up. It all started at the bus stop. We were near the playground, so the other kids played until this huge dusty yellow bus came. No one seemed to be in a rush to get on, but I wanted to find a good seat, so I was the first to step inside.

Is this the bus to primary school?

There was a kid behind me. "No, this is the bus to elementary school."

That's what I meant.

I went to the very back seat and it wasn't as wide as the other ones, so I knew I'd be able to sit by myself. Seconds later the rest of the kids crowded onto the bus, some of them voluntarily choosing to sit three to a seat. The smallest ones sat in the front. The ones my age aimed for the back. So, when they saw where I chose to sit, they weren't all that pleased. As usual, I didn't care. Not one bit. A girl asked me to move. Well, told me to move, and I said no. And the weirdest thing happened. She just settled her hands on the backs of the two seats in front of me and remained standing there. Even as the bus moved and headed down the main road, she stood there. The whole ride.

But once again – I didn't care. I even looked out the window to show her my indifference. I wasn't going to get into any fights – that was the plan. For my first day, that is.

And so by following the plan, I allowed my indifference to follow me throughout the whole school day. My morning class was Reading, but for forty-five minutes, Reading was interrupted by a class called "Specials." Monday's special was Gym. It was fun. The fat man that was supposedly a physical education expert had us play on the nets and ropes, telling us it was good for our upper body. Climbing was my specialty, so I ended up being one of the two kids in the class who made it to the very top of the rope. After that, I was called monkey. It wasn't the friendly way Adam had called me. It was in the same manner the kids said Lady Hurt. I ignored the desire to care.

After specials, we went back to Reading. Then there was lunch. We were assigned two tables in the cafeteria. There was a door in the room leading to outside, so with my plastic container of grapes and potato bread, I tried to leave. A grey-haired man with thick black glasses stopped me. I told him I was new and at my old school they let us go outside, so he just gave me a warning and I went back to the assigned table. I couldn't even go get a napkin from the table by the food line without permission. Even to stand I had to ask a lunch lady, it seemed. No one spoke to me. I heard a few whispers about the monkey trying to escape, but other than that, I didn't exist.

Recess followed lunch. It was my favorite part of the day. I was outside, and there were a bunch of footballs scattered across the blacktop to play with. I had my fun kicking the balls and trying to get them to hit the backboard of the basketball hoops. Rafael even joined me. We didn't really talk. We just played. That was fine with me.

Math was the finisher of the day. A paper with one hundred addition problems was placed in front of me and on the teacher's mark we had to complete all of them in the shortest amount of time possible. It wasn't my strongest subject, but I managed to finish before the slowest people.

School concluded and we were dismissed from our classrooms. We had to line up by bus and wait in the cafeteria for our bus number to be called. It was annoying how organized and limited everything was. The afternoon bus was more crowded than it was in the morning. We *all* had to sit three to a seat, and because I was pushed to the back of the line, I ended up squishing in with two first and second year girls. They looked maybe four or five. Kindergartners, they were called. It was a huge word to be associated with kids now beginning school. The girls took out dolls from their book bags and played on the top of the seat. No one messed with me, although I heard my monkey nickname being thrown about.

So it was a long first day. That night Mum and Dad wanted to know everything. I told them it was OK. That I was a fifth grader. That I made a friend. The last one was a lie, but it would give them peace of mind, and that was all I really wanted. Dad didn't look even remotely satisfied with my answers. Maybe something had happened at work. When bed time came around and I was finished my homework, I listened to Mum and Dad's bed discussion. I couldn't hear much, but I heard enough.

"She was lying. Right to your face. School was not OK."

"It'll get better. I'm sure it wasn't so bad."

"Woman, I know Ronnie. She's lying, and not for herself. She's lying for us."

I turned over in my sheets and tried to sleep.

School came and went after that. Each day seemed sort of the same, but not quite. Specials included Art, Science, Technology, and Music. Music and Gym became the things I looked forward to every week. Turns out I learned to love singing. When I sang with the other kids, I sounded just like them. It was like they didn't have their accents. It was like I didn't have an accent. We were all one voice.

My homeroom teacher, Mrs. Lakewood, always called on me to read things from papers, even if I didn't have my hand fully raised yet. I knew it was because she liked hearing me speak, she had the same facial expression as the taxi driver, but I pretended to believe her when she said it was only because I was such a good reader. She wasn't wrong. I read well. Sometimes when she asked what a particular word meant, like appalled, I was the only kid in the classroom who knew. I got glares from the other kids when I answered correctly. I thought I should dumb myself down, but I realized that, yes, being a know-it-all annoyed them, but being an anything annoyed them too, so might as well be a know-it-all.

Recess was a consistent type of fun. Rafael's class always came ten minutes into my class's recess time, and he always joined me for football. One day I asked where Kyle was. He told me Kyle was only a fourth grader. It made me happy.

Instead of sitting at my class-assigned table during lunch, I would sneak to Rafael's table and sit with him. He sat with two others boys and a girl. They all looked somewhat related. Maria, Carlos, and Ryan. Dark brown wavy hair and long eyelashes. Turns out they were triplets. I liked them. They never made me repeat what I said. Sometimes they said words I didn't know, like *almuerzo*, but I figured it out the more we spoke. I was learning Spanish.

Unlike my first day plan where I chose to be indifferent, my second day and every other day plan couldn't keep up. I started out to not care. Then it changed to pretending not to care. Then I began to care. I became an angry kid. I hit anyone who called me monkey to my face. I tripped people at recess when they bumped into me during their races, whether the bumps were accidental or not, I assumed they wouldn't be sorry for it anyways. I started aiming the footballs at kids I just didn't like at all. Lunch time was the only time I could be at ease.

My streak hit a bump when a fifth grader from my own class caught me with Rafael and our friends and told me to get back to the assigned table or else he'd tell on me. I called him a snitch and said nobody cares about me in my class, so why does he care now? As if my statement encouraged him to act on his threat, he raised his hand up high and began to call for the lunch lady.

And I punched him to the ground.

I got in trouble, but because the only people who witnessed the "fight" were my friends, I was let off easy. When there was a fight, the guidance counselor would gather the witnesses to write their "testimony" on a lined sheet of paper. I guessed all my witnesses liked me. All I got was a concerned phone call home.

Ms. Hurt was the one who got the message, but of course she relayed it to Mum and Dad. That day after school, Dad beat me until my bottom stung like I sat on an open flame.

"How does that feel, Ronnelle?"

Not good.

Yet I wasn't the only one getting angry. Dad was, too. At night he and Mum would continue their bed discussions until one would fall asleep. But then their bed discussions started to begin earlier and earlier in the day, until it was to the point where they would argue as soon as Dad got home from work and threw his bag on the bed. He always found something wrong. Something wrong with Mum. Something wrong with his work. Something wrong with me. It didn't help that my teacher sent me a note home saying that I needed to get more school supplies. All Dad saw on the paper was dollar signs, not a list of crayons and highlighters and scissors. There was apparently even something wrong with Uncle Johnny and Aunt Jemma. Anytime I asked about them, Dad would smack his palm against the wall and Mum would kindly tell me to go outside. "Selfish people. Selfish, selfish people," I'd hear Dad grumble when I made my escape.

I wasn't surprised Mum was being submissive. She had always been like that. Dad would get angry and raise his voice so loud you could hear it from the Spring Homes sign, yet Mum's voice remained hushed. Intense, but hushed. And that was how life was during the fall. Angry. We were all angry. Even Brendan seemed angry. To get away from the yelling, sometimes I took Brendan outside and we'd walk around a little, and when my arms got tired we'd sit on the curb. I still wasn't able to see Ms. Hurt. After all, she made it home before I did. Sometimes, though, if I got lucky, Ms. Hurt would peek her head out through her curtains on the second floor and we'd wave to one another. Well, I'd wave. Hers was more of a flick of the hand, but it counted a lot in my head.

An angry home was never a good one. As people changed, so did the things they did. Take me, for instance. As I got angrier, I ended up in more and more quarrels at school, whether it was simply screaming my head off with a girl who wouldn't stop mocking my voice, or pushing a kid down the slide because he was taking too long. Mum started cursing around the house. She had never cursed in front of me, ever. Dad, I was somewhat used to, but from Mum, bad words sounded strange. Things got so bad, Mum ended up sleeping in my bed with me. I was perfectly okay with it considering I liked the warmth, but that meant that Dad would be cold in his own bed.

Now, the new habit that Dad had gotten into was the most shocking. Mum cursing and fighting was nothing compared to this. One night, tucked in bed with Mum snoring by my head, I heard the bathroom door click and the sound of glass shattering. When I sat up and looked, I saw that the door wasn't completely shut, and Dad was definitely not in bed. So I slipped off my bed and made the meter walk to the bathroom door. As I knelt and peeked through the crack, for a moment I imagined myself in the step-house, peeking in Grandma's room, but the nostalgia ended as I saw Dad leaning over the sink. His breath sounded heavy as it poured out of his mouth.

He was crying. Not only that, there was glass all over the bathroom floor. It had to be the glass soap container. It was empty, probably empty for years. Dad had either done one of two things: knocked it over while he was crying, or worse, thrown it to the ground while he was crying. There was a difference.

I watched him bend over and pick up a shard. He placed it against his wrist, face cringing so much there were parallel lines on his profile. He shook. Then blood plipped to the ground.

I wanted to scream. I couldn't. It would wake Mum. Wake Brendan. Worst of all, it would make Dad realize I saw what he did, and I knew that would break him even more. I crawled back to bed and enveloped myself in the sheets. Except this time, I was in Dad's bed. Lonely, empty, and cold.

Tips

A mad household was no good for a ten-year-old who already had to deal with a new school, let alone a new country. It was no good. No good at all. To top it all off, we were well into fall and the cool air showed no partiality for those who were new to chilly weather. I found myself having to wear a sweater every day, even during recess. Well, at first I had that puffy black jacket, but seeing that the other kids wore things that were much thinner and easier to run in, I begged Mum to convince Dad to get me a sweater instead. Despite his grumbles and general aura of irritation, he bought me a yellow furry track sweater. It had a light brown stain on the front, but Mum worked her magic and got it to come off. I asked why the sweater came with a stain on it. I never really got an answer. I knew not to push it.

Wearing a sweater instead of a thick jacket meant that there was one less thing for the other kids at school to tease me about. They still teased and tested the waters, but I kept them in their place.

Well, I *had* kept them in their place. What with Dad's moods and Mum's silence and Brendan's constant whining, I felt like me getting into fights with kids at school all the time just added icing to the angry cake. To jam the squeeze bottle, things went from kids picking fights with me to kids wondering if I could even speak.

I was now the quiet girl. As much as I loved reading, I stopped raising my hand to read passages aloud. I stopped raising my hand altogether. When I was inevitably called on, I said as little words as possible. The less amount of time I was in the spotlight, the easier it was to avoid trouble. In math class I found out the measuring system here was completely different and much harder to visualize. I had trouble with relating feet to meters and inches to centimeters, but because I didn't say much I dodged a bullet. It would've been too easy for kids to figure out a way to turn me not knowing how to measure "properly" into a joke.

There were definitely times I was just ready to lose it, like when Christopher moved my chair from under me before I could sit down. I fell to my bottom and he laughed and the teacher wasn't in the classroom quite yet.

I wanted to throw my seat at him and call him what my Dad called Mum the other night, but I didn't because I remembered why I was being calm in the first place.

And just when I thought I was getting the hang of being Renewed Ronnelle, a fault would always be brought to the table to make it difficult once again. Some of my classmates started noticing that my outfits were repeating pretty often. It wasn't like it was purposeful. I lost some weight and I got a little taller so my old shirts were fitting loose and fitting shorter. I resorted to wearing the new shirts Dad bought me, and there weren't a whole lot to choose from. Jamie started it – the whole "dirty Ronnie" trend. Anytime another kid repeated their outfit, they were considered a dirty Ronnie for the day. An honor, really. Yet I kept my cool and let the names fling around. I still had hope. I had Rafael and Maria and Carlos and Ryan. The only name calling I got from any of them was from Maria, and she called me *bella*. I didn't know completely what it meant, but I knew it was good by the look of her smile.

The after school situation wasn't an improvement, though. I still never could manage to get a seat with Rafael. Kyle always clung to him on the bus, and they'd always end up sitting with a third person before I could dare to venture to the back. So I remained with the two kindergartners and their dolls. Occasionally they offered me a turn, but only to guest star as a crazy relative. I didn't mind; they were sweet girls and I got them to laugh a lot. It made me happy. *Bella* and kindergarten giggles made me so happy.

What also made me happy was when I found money lying around throughout the school grounds and my neighborhood. It was strange how often people got careless and lost their change. I would never, ever lose my money, and I knew my parents were on the same boat. Kids whose parents trusted them with a few dollars for lunch money would lose some of it and it'd end up happily in my hands. I wasn't bad about it. I made sure to wait until after all lunch shifts ended before I allowed myself to pick up money. Thanks to my little collections, every now and then I'd take a walk to the post office, which was within walking distance like everything else in Scottsville, and get a free envelope from the nice lady at the desk. I'd tuck the earnings I accumulated into the envelope, write *"Tips for Jessica"* on the front, and drop it in the tip jar at Whitman's. I wanted to be anonymous because I knew she didn't want to take anything from me, so I didn't ever sign my name, and I didn't ever let Mr. Steve see me. Dropping the envelope in the tip jar made me feel good.

I liked to find things that made me happy because at night Mum still slept in bed with me and Brendan slept alone in his crib with a little pout on his face and Dad would be in the bathroom with a shard of glass positioned against his wrist. I knew because at night I'd survey the room and Dad's bed would be empty. Untouched. I'd slither off of bed as to not wake Mum, which was easy considering her snoring never quit, and peek through the bathroom doorway. Dad didn't shut the door all the way because I knew he knew I was always a light sleeper and the bathroom door shutting could shoot my eyes open during the loudest of dreams. I slept through Mum's snoring because Mum's snoring was home and I was familiar with that sound to the point where it would probably call for a restless night for me if she *didn't* snore. On the other hand, the excruciating silence of Dad alone in the bathroom making himself bleed could wake me up and keep me up. It was happening routinely, but I didn't want to ignore it and let myself sleep. I didn't want it to become home. One day I split my street money and picked up two envelopes. Half went to Whitman's tip jar, especially signed as *"Tips for Jessica."* The other half was slipped under Dad's pillow. *"Tips for the Papers."*

I never found out if Dad opened the envelope or recognized my handwriting because it was never brought up. It didn't seem to change anything. But something did change the next day. We were all in our typical positions for dinner – Mum, Dad, and I sitting in a sort of triangle on the floor while Brendan relaxed on my bed. We were eating subs. Mum and I split a *twelve-inch* sub and Dad had split a second for himself. The remaining half went in the fridge. As we ate in silence, the sound of a door slamming upstairs could just barely be heard. Ms. Hurt had come home. She didn't have to work a double that Friday. I didn't know if that was a good sign or not. But then the sound of a door erupted again, except it was closer. A doorknob jingled. The sound ceased and all went quiet. Mum and Dad didn't worry about it and we continued our evening as if nothing happened.

Yet at bed time, when Mum was in my bed and Dad was in the bathroom, I found myself at the top of the basement staircase where the door was. Curious, I placed my hand on the knob and twisted. And the door actually opened.

I didn't dare step inside. I shut the door back and went straight to bed, not worrying too much about Dad that night. All I could think about as I tried to fall asleep was that I now had the ability to walk into Ms. Hurt's home if I wanted. I knew this was a good sign.

Mum's Choice

It was no surprise I continued to have trouble sleeping. I mean, I always had some degree of trouble sleeping no matter how comfy I felt at the time. I still have a little trouble sleeping today. Nothing was really getting better in the Hurt basement besides the somewhat amusing fact that the name Dad gave the basement began to truly match.

I thought maybe Mum began to notice that Dad was in the habit of cutting himself considering it left visible marks on his arm. Yes, he wore long-sleeve button-ups to work, so no one at the cell phone company would notice, but at home he was quick to switch into his puffy sweatpants and a T-shirt. She had to have noticed. They didn't sleep together but they still lived together.

And they sure did argue together, too.

So *that* could be the reason she said nothing about it. They were too busy arguing, and the arguments were getting dumber and dumber by the day. I thought they were going crazy. I had quit putting up a fight at school because I hoped it would do something, but it didn't do anything at all. In fact, I don't think they even noticed there were no longer any phone calls home.

But like all good things, all bad things come to an end. I had reached a milestone – my first report card in an *elementary* school. I had to get it signed to prove to my homeroom teacher that I showed my parents. She stressed it to the class and then later again to me because "things may be different" where I'm from. I told her she didn't have to worry – I wanted to show my parents my straight A's. When I got home that day, I kept my report card in my transparent book bag and under my bed until Dad came home.

I remember it pretty vividly. As soon as I heard the doorknob sing I dived for my report card and placed it on my pedestal of a bed. I was so excited I took Brendan from Mum without really having a reason to. Doing that got Mum's attention, so it didn't take long for her to notice the envelope with my name printed on it. She reached for it, and I was ready to accept some well-deserved compliments, but Dad opened his mouth before anything could happen.

"You see me step in the house and don't say anything? Not a good evening? Not a, how was work today, honey? You just shoot me a glance? What does a man got to do to get some love around here?"

Now, I understood Dad's point to some extent, but he wasn't really in the basement long enough to see if Mum would say anything. He was-

"-jumping to conclusions. Why you always jumping to conclusions, Sean?"

There we go. I watched as the report card in Mum's hand slowly found its way back on the bed. Great. The moment was over, not that the moment even started.

"Jumping to conclusions? You never say good-anything to me when I get home from a long day of dealing with idiots who think America is the only place where cell phones are a growing industry! I don't hear nothing from you, woman. Nothing!"

"If you just gave me a chance! Oh gosh boy if you just gave me a chance! The minute you step your tired foot in here, hell breaks loose. You give me no time to say anything nice. No time, and no chance! You're an angry, angry man, Sean."

"Well you're a-"

"Angry, angry woman. Hell yeah, you surely got that right. I'm sick of this."

"I'm sick, too! Damn right I is sick! You spend the day hugging up your son while I'm working, working ,working to get food in this place."

"Sean! That is bull! You're the one who told me to stay home. You're the one who said to let you handle the money for now. You. You! And now you're-"

Mum suddenly stopped speaking as I held Brendan closer to my chest. Despite all the yelling, Brendan stared straight up at my face as if he didn't know hell was "breaking loose." As if hell breaking loose was home to him.

"Sean," Mum said, her voice quiet. Her facial expression softened. She was thinking about something. She didn't look angry anymore. She didn't look angry at all.

"What?" Dad said. His voice was still loud as ever, but it cracked like he was getting caught for doing something wrong.

And apparently he was, because the next thing Mum said was:

"I know exactly what you're up to."

After that statement, the pause button on the argument was pushed and the attention went back to my report card again. It was weird. Mum took the envelope and made a big show of opening it up. Her eyes traveled down as she read each letter grade. She then held it up towards Dad and he snatched it and his eyes did the same.

"Straight A's? Our Ronnie's a child genius!" Dad hooted and tossed the card on the bed.

So my parents congratulated me and gave me a high-five and for dinner that night Dad left and came back with warm bowls of store-bought cream of potato soup. I never had cream of anything soup because back home we never went fancy with the broth. We did your basic chicken broth and tossed in whatever vegetables and meat we felt. Pig toe. Ox tail. Chicken breast. It was fun because there were so many variations. But the cream of potato was delicious and I remember having the weird sensation that there was milk in the soup. I felt sick to my tummy afterward and spent quite a while on the toilet that evening.

After the vomit I still had a heavy feeling in my stomach. I felt as though the fight couldn't have been over. Did I imagine it all? Why were things going so smoothly?

The answers arrived before the day completely ended. At bed time, Mum didn't go in my bed. She went in hers. I really thought I was going crazy. I slipped in my bed and tried to sleep, I really did, but I couldn't. Not necessarily because of the weird events that day, but because I couldn't hear Mum's snoring, meaning she wasn't really asleep. Then I heard Mum and Dad's soft voices and I shut my eyes tight.

"She's asleep."

"Let's go in the bathroom just in case."

Light footsteps fluttered across the cold basement floor. Since the bathroom door was only a few *feet* away from my bed, my heart stopped as Mum and Dad passed by. I heard their breathing and it felt so close, but I had to keep my face relaxed or else they'd know. When I heard the bathroom door shut, I slid off my bed and crawled to the door, my ear already settled against it.

"You want me out, don't you?" Mum.

"What do you mean, woman? Don't get me wrong, if you want to leave, I'm not holding you-"

"Sean, stop right there. I know what you're doing. You know that I know. So stop it right now, because it's never going to happen."

"What do you think I'm doing? This isn't a game, Kim. I want respect-"

"I'll tell you what you want. You want me to leave. You want me to divorce you."

"That's not what-" Silence. "That's not really what I want."

"It's not what you want, but it's what you're hoping for, ent?"

Silence. A long, long silence. So long my eyelids began to fall on their own will.

"You didn't marry a fool, Sean."

"I know. But you did."

"No I didn't."

"Yes you did. Look where we are. Look at what we've been eating. We're caged in here. I still have to get these papers through and through. Ronnie's got it tough at school, I know she does. I know you wish you can go out and work but we can't afford to leave Brendan anywhere. I tried to update my driver's license and it was completely shut down. Denied. I'm a fool, Kim, I'm a fool."

I pictured Dad sitting on the closed toilet seat with his hands running through his dark wavy hair.

"You're not a fool, Sean. A fool is someone who does foolishness. Foolishness didn't bring us here."

"It doesn't even matter what brought us here anymore. We're here. I don't like coming home and seeing you look so bored. I don't like that we don't have a stove, or that our fridge is never full. I don't like that you're stuck here."

"I'm not stuck here. I could leave if I wanted to. Marry an American citizen. Skip the process and get citizenship just like that. Bring our kids, too. Sounds wonderful."

"Then, please, Kim, just do it. It'll be easy. You're young and beautiful. Those men at the shoe store couldn't stop looking at you. Just-"

"Do you honestly think a bunch of petty, stupid arguments will drive me away? You're giving everything you can to keep us alive and healthy."

"Don't you want a full kitchen? And a house and a husband who can-"

"Shut up with that stupidness right this second and listen to me very carefully."

Silence.

"I am never, ever leaving your side. Do you hear me?"

More silence.

"And another thing. Don't you ever cut your skin again. That's not the skin I married."

I felt like I had heard enough because another silence followed that demand and my eyelids were falling again and getting harder to open back up. I stood and wobbled over to Brendan's crib. I scooped him up in my arms and placed him on my parents' bed. Then I got into that bed as well and stared at my little brother's round face. His features were really setting in. His hair was going to be long and curly and shiny like mine and Mum's, but he was going to have a wide nose like Dad for sure.

I cared a lot about what happened that night. I cried quietly beside Brendan. His sleeping comforted me. He was lucky. He had no idea what was going on. Sometimes I tried to lead myself to believe that he knew what was happening, but I think I just didn't want to feel alone in this. I was somewhere in the middle between clueless and up-to-date. I didn't have any idea what exactly these "papers" did, or what they meant, but I knew their effect on us. I only knew how things affected my family, and I'm not sure if this knowledge was good or bad to have.

But like I said earlier, all bad things, like good things, come to an end. That night, the stop button was pushed, not the pause button, and I knew that Mum and Dad's scream-offs would never have to be accepted as my home.

Tips Returned

Winter was a brutal, brutal time. I definitely put my oversized jacket to use by the end of fall. It's ironic how the coldest time of year was equivalent to the hottest place in the universe: hell. The basement became even colder at night. I always wore socks, but during the winter I found myself wearing my sweater or keeping a blanket wrapped around my shoulders in my own home. November seemed to be over in an angry blink. A national holiday passed – Thanksgiving – but obviously we didn't do anything for it. I had watched videos in school about it during classes and it seemed like a nice holiday. We got some days off of school. When I got back, I was hoping to hear cool Thanksgiving stories of other kids dressed up as turkeys and pilgrims and Indians and talking about the things their family said they were thankful for, but all they told me was that they ate a ton of food.

Winter wasn't a complete let down, though. Good things were happening as I shivered and saw my breath in a weird smoky form in front of my lips. While the weather outside got colder, the tension at home cooled down. Mum and Dad's fights were rare and never so serious. They even teased one another and touched each other's shoulders when they passed. I thought it was gross, but I knew this was a good sign. Mum would look at me and tell me to fix my face before she "fixes it for me." Brendan became noticeably happy, too. He laughs and smiles without any reason to. One time while I was reading a school book with Brendan resting next to me in my bed, I put my hand towards him to poke his fat face and he immediately snapped his gums over my finger. Of course I yanked my hand away and glared at him, but he just stared right at my wet hand and laughed. He was evil when he was ready.

School didn't change very much. Nothing got worse, thankfully, besides the fact that we couldn't go outside for recess anymore until it got warm again. I still sat with the two little girls in the front of the bus. I still got avoided and teased for whatever reason the other kids could find, like when I confused Mr. Forb by describing Abraham Lincoln as "long" instead of "tall." I didn't know why people found that so funny, but I decided not to make that mistake again. And of course, the term "dirty Ronnie" continued throughout the year because I still had to keep repeating outfits.

Yet I also sat with my friends during lunch and learned Spanish words like *gringos* and made funny jokes about the lunch lady and her little round glasses. I started reading aloud in class again and writing the answers to math problems on the chalkboard. Rafael and I walked home together and started holding hands to keep them warm. We both had our own gloves and our own pockets, but holding hands was better. I can't remember who took the other's hand first. Maybe it was me. Maybe not.

Throughout the season there was still something on my mind that wouldn't go away. Ms. Hurt had no car and never took a taxi to get home, meaning she just had to walk. I mean, I had to walk home too, but my distance was shorter and I had a friend with me. Ms. Hurt had to walk a little longer, and she was alone. She had to walk longer and alone in her yellow top and skirt and apron. She did have a nice black jacket that went to her knees, and I noticed her legs were much darker than her skin, so she must have had stockings on as well. Her hood had fur lining the edges, but the hood itself wasn't big enough for all her hair to fit, so curly red strands popped out while the rest was being compressed by the fabric. Her head looked big and oddly shaped. I knew all of this because I peeked out the house one Sunday afternoon to look out for her. She spotted me at the side of her house in no time, but we didn't say anything. We didn't have to. We were friends already. She just offered a flick of her hand and I waved in return, and then we went to our separate homes.

Actually, it was that very day that the basement door went from being simply unlocked to *open*. I was eating a cluster of grapes after dinner when I heard a sound from upstairs. We all walked to the bottom of the basement stairs and looked up, and instead of seeing a door, we saw a white wall with a framed picture of a little red head and an old woman. It could've just been me, but my night's sleep that evening felt warmer as if the heat from upstairs was able to somehow reach me.

Given the way things were going, I wasn't all that surprised when Dad threw off his shoes *and* socks one day and said it was time for our next chapter.

Chapter four!

Dad started putting his socks back on. It was too cold to keep them off, even if his news was wonderful. "Four? Now how'd you come up with that number?"

The number of homes we've had. The next will be our fourth one.

Mum emerged from the bathroom asking us what all the bacchanal was about. Dad repeated everything that was said and then Mum turned to me seriously.

"Four? Now, we'll have four living arrangements, but we will always have *one* home, and it's going to stay that way. Alright?"

I nodded. One home. Got it.

Dad kept staring at me funny. "I thought you'd be more surprised than this. Did you know we were moving?"

I shrugged. It wasn't like this was the first time we just up and left our home. I had a feeling Mum and Dad made their own plans. They were just waiting for a day to spring up the news. So, I was waiting too. Afraid of sounding too smart, I didn't say anything.

"Well, we're leaving tomorrow morning. Tonight we'll pack our things. I got a van we can borrow to put all our stuff in and move to the apartment."

"Oh, where'd you get a van?"

"Larry."

"That man has been helping us a lot. When I get my new kitchen tomorrow we'll invite him over for dinner some time. Is he driving?"

"Nah, he said I could do it."

"Does he know you don't have...?"

"He knows. The way people drive up here on these easy wide roads? A license says nothing about driving skill. Nothing. Them tiny swirly roads back home will kill them all." Dad laughed and dropped himself on his bed.

116

Mum followed him, lying herself flat across the sheets. I snuggled between them while Brendan sat in his crib with a pacifier tucked in his mouth.

Will I be going to a new school?

"No. The apartment complex is not far from here. There's a bus stop for your school down there, too. Playground. Lots of kids. A big empty field you could play football in."

"And we can finally invite friends over," Mum added.

"Well, first you got to make some friends, Kim."

Mum smacked Dad on the arm and we all laughed a little. As far as we knew, Mum's only friend was Brendan.

"I'll be sure to invite the lady from the shoe store."

We all laughed again, but then Ms. Hurt came to my mind. She'd be alone in the house again. I wouldn't be there to stop kids from bugging her from afar. I wouldn't be there to drop off my floor money.

Does Ms. Hurt know?

"Of course she knows. I let her know last Saturday when I found the apartment. This week I worked everything out with Larry and he and I got a couple things done." Dad sounded like he was talking to Mum instead of me, but at least my question was answered.

"Oh, Sean. Ms. Hurt said we could leave through the front door."

"What? That'll just make things harder."

"Well we can pack the van through our door, and then after we'll leave through the front. She insisted, Sean. She's done so much for us – she even lowered rent, remember? Let's just do what she asked."

Ms. Hurt lowered rent? I wondered why.

"You're right." Dad sat up. "Let's get most of our stuff packed tonight and see what happens in the morning."

Chapter Four is coming soon!

"Chapter Four," Mum repeated. She closed her eyes and spoke all dreamlike. "Four is a nice number, don't you think, Sean?"

For a Sunday, morning was a hustle. We woke up and cleaned up and bundled up. We packed away the remaining things we didn't pack the night before because we still had to use them, like toothbrushes and bedsheets. A horn beeped outside and Dad said that was Larry. We took our suitcases and grocery bags of food from the fridge and left. Mum stayed inside to finish putting Brendan's coat on. The zipper had been stuck.

Outside there were two vehicles, a blue pickup truck and a white van. A man with white pants and a shiny leather jacket that didn't look warm enough to prevent him from getting goosebumps was leaning against the van.

"Star boy!" Dad said, and there was more life in his step. They slapped hands and gave each other the classic manly one-arm hug. "Thanks again, Larry."

"Anything for you, Sean, anything for you."

His voice sounded like home. Larry was one of us. I stared at him, almost dropping the grocery bags from my grasp. I was wearing the red and black climbing gloves Dad got me ages ago.

"Larry, this is my daughter, Ronnelle. Ronnie, this is Larry."

"Call me Uncle Larry, Ronnie Nose." He pulled out a tissue from his pocket and handed it to me.

Embarrassed, I accepted the tissue and dabbed at my nose. He was definitely worthy of being called an uncle. Uncles always gave you odd nicknames, but that was their way of affection.

Hi, Uncle Larry.

"Never trust a man in a real big white van unless he's your uncle, okay Nose?" Uncle Larry smiled at me and then patted my dad on the back. "Alright, got to run now. Me and the boys are liming before church."

"Aye-aye, don't go too crazy. It's Sunday."

They laughed and laughed. They laughed as Larry got into the passenger seat of the pickup and Dad started packing the van. They laughed as the blue truck zoomed away and Dad marched back into the basement. Mum was already ready with Brendan buckled in his crib.

"I knew having a car seat as a crib would come in handy," Dad joked.

We all climbed the stairs to the open door at the top. It was all so weird for me. I never bothered to even step on the bottom step before. I was the happiest girl in the world. When I reached the top, I took one long look at the photograph framed on the wall across from us. It was no doubt Ms. Hurt and her grandmother. That was good to see – she hadn't always been alone.

We took a left and walked down a narrow hallway with a wall on one side and a staircase leading to the second floor on the other. It was too bad Ms. Hurt was at work. I wanted to say bye and good luck.

The hallway led straight to the front door. Dad unlocked it and opened it wide. He made a comment about how good this all felt. I looked over my shoulder to try and peek at more of the house. It was so empty. In the foyer there was just a doormat and a thin door that was probably a closet. To the left was the opening to the living room, but all I could see from my angle was a floral couch that reminded me of Mrs. Sadd's house dress.

But then to my right was a small room with a tall window and a chandelier. There was a small, wooden round table with four chairs surrounding it. A breakfast room. It was a breakfast room. Sitting nicely on top of the table were four leaf-patterned placemats. In the center was a fruit basket, but I knew even from my distance that the fruits were plastic.

A familiar envelope was lying at the edge of the table.

Hey!

I rushed to the table and picked up the envelope. It was the one I got from the post office. I knew because across the front my hand-written words were still scribbled on it. "Tips for Jessica."

But Jessica was crossed out. Written above it in neat cursive was my name.

Tips for Ronnie.

"Quit snooping around before I bus' yuh tail!" Mum yelled from the front door.

I stuffed the envelope in my front pocket and ran out the door. Soon we all piled into the van. It was spacious and I didn't need to fight to see out the window because we all got our own end seat. Mum and Dad sat in the front while Brendan and I had our own seats in the middle. As we pulled off and began to drive away from the house, I glanced back, my eyes instinctively being drawn to the second story window. Of course, no one was there. Ms. Hurt was at work. I looked forward again when the van suddenly jerked forward and Mum scolded Dad for driving on the wrong side of the road. He giggled and moved to the right side. As our speed steadied I pulled out the envelope again.

Tips for Ronnie. I opened it and peered inside. There was a single fifty-dollar bill. I took it out and revealed a smaller piece of paper behind it. She wrote in cursive.

"Turns out your tips added up to exactly $50. Don't give out your money so freely or else you'll end up stuck like me."

My thumb slid against the bill in my hand. I never held one worth so much. She could've used it.

"You've been good to me, Ronnie."

I shoved the money and note back into the envelope and tucked it away in my pocket again. Turning my head to the house that was slowly disappearing from sight, I felt the need to cry again. The Hurt basement wouldn't be ours anymore. I was upset that she didn't accept my money, money that she needed and said she needed.

But even more so, I was sad that I couldn't go back and put the envelope back where I found it. As we turned the corner, I looked to the second story window again and saw that it was open.

Ms. Hurt was never at work that morning.

Part Three

Home

Sky Dandruff

From my point of view, the move to the apartment was easy. The drive was maybe ten minutes and the entrance was beautiful. On either side of the road was a bed of red and yellow pansies, the flowers that look like little lion faces. In the middle of the road where the yellow paint streak would be was a strip of grass with a sign that read "Scapeview Apartments." The complex was huge. There were roads branching off of the main one, all leading to different loops of apartment buildings. The buildings all looked the same. Brown and red bricks with a purple awning with the building number on it. When we pulled up to a building with the number four on the front I wanted to laugh. I was thinking of Ms. Hurt standing by her window watching us leave, but seeing that number reminded me that we had to move on to the next chapter like Dad said. Ms. Hurt was still stuck in her own chapter.

We entered the building. It wasn't that tall, only three floors. The hallway was barely lit by a flickering ceiling light and the stairs were rubbery and black. I followed after Mum and Dad. Apparently our new "living arrangement" was on the very top floor. It took just two trips to get all of our stuff to the door. Dad made a big show of pulling out his keys from his pocket. He opened the door slowly, as if it wasn't our apartment at all and he didn't want to wake whoever was inside.

No one was inside, though, but all our furniture was. We had a living room with two dirt-brown couches and a bright orange puffy chair. There was a cubic television against the wall and I dropped my plastic bag to touch it.

This is ours?

"That's right, crapaud," Dad answered, pulling the suitcases inside. Mum placed Brendan's car seat on the couch and went straight toward the kitchen.

I didn't know apartments come with furniture.

"Besides kitchen and bathroom appliances, everything in here – I had it all set up and ready for moving day. Check out the rest of the place, baby girl."

I didn't really care to move from the television. It was mine. It was ours. We had our own television and our own remote control. There wasn't a NES, but I shrugged it off and stood to my feet. Mum screamed from the kitchen. Dad and I rushed to her, both of us asking in panic if she was alright. And she was. She had a big grin on her face and Brendan started laughing.

"I love my kitchen! I love my kitchen! I can cook again! I'm making dinner tonight!"

Dad chuckled and told me to go see my room. I ran to it without wasting a second. At the end of the short hallway was my doorway. When I stepped inside, I lost the ability to keep still. I had a skinny wooden bed with a pink pillow and matching comforter that had a cartoony white lady with pink lips and blue eyes all over the fabric. A Barbie themed bed set. I never liked Barbie, never had the chance to, but now I looked like a huge fan. On the opposite wall was a wooden crib. A real crib, not a car seat. There was a black blanket rolled up at the edge. I suddenly felt so happy for Brendan. He was definitely too young to appreciate having an actual bed, but I knew he was smart enough to notice that his sleeping arrangement had upgraded.

Between our beds was a window. I peered through the blinds. The view was of the playground in the back, as well as a hill and a portion of the field Dad had mentioned. There were no kids out. It was too cold.

The room also had drawers and a closet, and leaning against the closet was a full-length pink mirror with a crack in the corner. I stared at my reflection. I looked like a marshmallow in my jacket. I laughed and laughed and as I looked at the mirror again, I finally noticed the floor.

Carpet. We had carpet. I flung my boots and socks off and ran through the house, loving the feeling of the ground absorbing each step.

Mum and Dad emerged from the room next to mine, their room, and yelled at me to stop running. Living above people meant that I couldn't run or jump. I didn't run or jump all that much in any of our old houses, but now that it was a rule, I felt restricted.

But hey, we had carpet.

I wanted to roll around and crawl and slide my socks against the ground to see if I could shock someone and play around with the television and sit at the dining table and hop over the kitchen counter and open and close our fridge and turn our stove on and jump on my bed and Brendan's bed and Mum and Dad's bed and hide in my closet and look at myself in the mirror. I wished that Brendan could talk so that we could go on and on about our new home. Instead I listened to Dad explain the things near us that we could do.

"There's a swimming pool and a laundromat just outside here. G.W. is even closer to here than the Hurt basement, too."

"Is that where you got the couches?" Mum asked.

"Yeah."

"I can tell."

My parents chuckled. We had the blinds of the dining room window open, and something caught my eyes.

Is it raining outside now?

Mum turned around and Dad simply turned his head, both squinting their eyes to the window I was staring at.

Does the rain here fall slower?

"No…"

I can't remember who answered me.

We all stood at the exact same time and rushed to the window. Dad raised the blinds so we could see better. It wasn't rain. Rain was transparent and fell so fast that sometimes you couldn't see it, just hear it. This, this you couldn't hear at all, but you could see it very easily. It was white and yes it was falling, but it was moving in a wiggly path at the mercy of the wind, as if it were lighter than water.

"It's snow!" Mum exclaimed.

When I turned to her voice, she was gone and I heard the front door slam. Dad followed after her, but not before telling me to put my coat back on and leave the door unlocked. I did as he said. It's funny how a task as simple as slipping on a jacket could turn into something as complicated as solving a Rubik's cube when you're dying to get it done. My hands kept fumbling through the sleeves, and the zipper got stuck halfway up. Finally I finished bundling up and galloped down the rubbery stairs to my family outside.

This was snow. Mum was twirling around as the white fluff floated downward towards the earth. It stuck to our coats and hair and Dad's long eyelashes. Brendan's mouth was hanging open and his nose quickly turned red. Snow accumulated on the sidewalk, a thin layer I could dust off with my foot. It made the ground sparkle when the sunlight hit it. It was a white carpet, except it was for the outdoors.

"It looks like little crumbs are falling off the clouds," Dad said as he collected some snow in his hands.

"Or dandruff," Mum said as she snuggled Brendan up to her cheek.

I copied Dad by holding my hand in front of me to see if I could catch some. The snow was cold and melted quickly. I couldn't get a good look at it. I wanted to see how the flakes would look up close. In drawings, they were pretty and made of a bunch of diamonds and arrows, but here, all I could see was fuzz. Now, I'd seen snow before, but seeing it in pictures and cartoons and movies did not qualify as actually seeing it at all. This is what winter brought our family. A new home for our home, and snow.

I stuck my tongue out to taste the sky dandruff.

Larry

It didn't take very long for me to get used to calling Uncle Larry, *Uncle* Larry. I mean, it wouldn't be the first time I called someone "uncle." It was a sign of respect and closeness. You would call a family friend your uncle. It was just what we did. Plus, I liked Uncle Larry. He was funny and he dressed like a star boy and he just treated us right. It was also refreshing to speak with him. I hadn't met anyone here who spoke like us besides Uncle Larry.

Uncle Larry made every effort to be with us. Basically, it seemed like he was everywhere. He wasn't there-there, but he was there.

Let me explain. The white van he lent us on moving day didn't disappear after moving day. Dad borrowed it all the time after that. He no longer took a taxi to work and back. Now, he didn't have a license, but he didn't let that "minor detail" stop him. He never ever got a ticket before, and according to him, moving to another country won't change his record. Mum said he was being foolish and that there was a first for everything, especially since we were in a new country, but Dad brushed it off. Mum and I didn't bother him too much after that. Watching him drive around, he looked so happy. So satisfied. Each day when he got home from work, he'd blow the horn of the van, two happy beeps. I'd run to my window and open it and wave, and he'd salute back. I wondered where he got that gesture from. He hadn't done it before.

But then my wonder came to an end. Uncle Larry dropped by at least four times a week. He'd come over and eat with us, and when he left for the evening, he'd salute right before door shuts. Uncle Larry wasn't a long-eyed leech, though. He didn't always come over and expect food to be given to him. Sometimes Mum cooked and he'd accept food, other times when she offered, he'd say no. There were also nights where he'd bring a bag of plastic bowls from his house, all filled with food. One night, I remember, he brought us a feast. Fried rice with vegetables. Callaloo. Stewed chicken. Cucumber salad. It was a meal fit for a Sunday, but it was only a Wednesday.

"An unmarried man has every right to eat like he's married," he said when all of our eyes caught the bag in his hand.

That day, Mum turned off the stove (she had put up water to boil) and we all dived in. Uncle Larry could cook. He was welcome any time.

Eventually I noticed a few weird things that made questions spring up in my mind again, but these weren't things that worried me. Just confused me. For instance, the day I took home my perfect scored math test, Mum gave me a little key and told me to get our mail from downstairs. I did as she said, taking a few extra seconds to slide down the railing, and popped open our mail door. There wasn't much mail, which wasn't a surprise, but as I walked back to our apartment door, I noticed that all of the skinny envelopes didn't have our name on it. They all read "Larry Dubois." I gave Mum the mail. She noticed me staring at the name even as I handed the envelopes to her, but when we finally made eye contact, I didn't ask anything. By then, I was used to not knowing exactly what was going on at home, but as long as we survived, I chose not to care. Grandma had taught me that.

I have to admit, I did have a few occasions where I really wanted to ask what was going on, like when Mum and Dad were talking and Dad suddenly remembered that he had to "send Larry the money" because the "month is almost over." But again, I didn't let my curiosity kill me. When I found pieces of broken glass in the bathroom cabinet behind the mirror, I didn't let my curiosity kill me then, either.

Uncle Larry ended up giving Dad the van as an early Christmas gift. He said he had been meaning to give it away because he had no use for it. I thought it was the coolest thing. Not necessarily receiving a van, but knowing someone who could easily *give away* a van.

So Uncle Larry had every right to be called Uncle Larry. He was my Dad's best friend. His only friend, as far as I knew. He helped Dad move our furniture in the house. He cooked dinner for us. He brought wine for Mum and Dad and a bottle of pineapple juice for me. He made Brendan laugh. He gave us a van. I thought it was an honor that our mail arrived under his name.

My favorite memory of Uncle Larry was when he came over on a Sunday night with dark red wine, pineapple juice, and a plastic container of cut up mangos. We drank and ate curried shrimp for dinner, and afterwards we dug in to the mangos. I hadn't had mangos in a long, long time. The ones I ate that day weren't nearly as good as the ones from Adam's tree, but they were still a treat. Each piece reminded me of home.

"Where do you get your mangos from?" Dad asked.

"The produce market. Owned by a real nice family. Guatemalans. Real nice fruit."

"I can make a mango chow. I haven't made that in a long time," Mum commented.

"Aye, make me some chutney, Kimmy. I real miss chutney. Mam used to make it for me back home," Uncle Larry said.

Uncle Larry, do you miss home?

"Sure, Ronnie Nose."

"But it's weird, ent? Not living on an island. Not knowing the ocean is only a few miles away," Dad said. He then put on his writer-face. Tongue wiping his top front teeth and eyebrows stressing to reach his nose. It was the face he made when he was thinking hard.

"Everywhere is an island. Some are bigger than others, I guess." Uncle Larry looked at his wrist despite there being no watch located there. He rose. We had finished the mangos and were just sitting around with our happy tummies. He picked up his plastic bowl and covered it. It was his sign that he had to start heading home. "I may not have family on this island, but I've got family on the next one." Then he wished for us to have a good week and saluted the second before the door closed him from view.

And that's why I still love Uncle Larry, even if he's old and grumpy and requires a tube to get some air. He taught me that no matter where I was on the planet, I was still on an island.

Brand Oreos

Winter was not a discreet season, not at all. The snow, as exciting as it was the first couple times, went from cute and chilly to just plain cold. Instead of floating in little tufts, it came down like obese cotton balls. It climbed up my coat sleeves and gave me shivers that lingered even after the snow was removed off my skin. It also left a thick layer of semi-transparent greyness over sidewalks and streets. Mum didn't like me going outside. I asked her why, and when she took me out to stand on the sidewalk, I knew why. It truly felt like you were standing on a buttery ice cube.

The perk about moving not too far from my previous "living arrangement" was that I didn't have to switch schools, meaning I didn't have to meet new kids and try to make friends again. I didn't have to start over. Sure, I was sad that I couldn't ride the bus with Rafael (even though we never really got to sit with each other all that much) or walk home with him, but the new bus I rode still had its perk. Actually, it had three perks. Triplets. Maria, Carlos, and Ryan were excited the day I stepped on their bus. The bus, unlike my last one, wasn't packed and smelly, and the kids weren't really separated by their individual forms. Kindergartners sat with first-graders, second-graders sat with fifth-graders. The triplets sat somewhere in the middle. Carlos and Ryan sat with each other on their one dark green seat, and Maria sat in the seat across from them. Now I got to sit beside her, and everything was fair.

A lot of people make the mistake of thinking that you have to be alone to be lonely, but that wasn't really the case. A whole group of people, ironically, could feel lonely. One time at lunch I tried to convince the triplets and Rafael that we were all lonely, but they insisted we weren't.

"I'm never lonely. *Nunca*," Carlos said.

"Me neither. How can you say we feel lonely when you're using the word *we*?" Maria asked.

It made no sense to her, or any of them for that matter, but I knew what I was talking about. We were lonely. They didn't get harassed like I did, but they were lonely too. I didn't see them hang out with other kids besides me. Ryan even admitted one day (and the others agreed) that the only people he likes at school are us and Mrs. Greene, the pretty art teacher who always had chopsticks stabbed into her hair bun like someone incorrectly eating a dumpling. We were lonely kids and I was fixed on trying to make them accept it.

That same day, within that half hour, we all took out our snacks to see if we wanted to trade anything. Rafael had vanilla pudding. Carlos and Ryan had a brownie. Maria took out a bag of sandwich cookies. Each cookie was really two black cookies glued together with white icing.

"Yes, Oreos!" Maria squealed.

I have Oreos too!

I took out a plastic bag of my own cookies.

"Let's trade," Maria suggested with a playful giggle.

We all laughed as I handed Maria one of my Oreos for one of hers. I was about to stuff her cookie in my mouth when I noticed her stare at mine. The one I gave her.

"This isn't an Oreo," Maria said. She held up two cookies in front of my face. The left was hers and the right was mine. The left was darker and had "OREO" inscribed into the cookie like a coin, meanwhile mine had no writing at all. Just a punch of jagged lines on a manhole cover.

Still, I defended my cookie. When Dad brought home the package, he told me they were Oreos. He wouldn't just lie to my face.

These are Oreos. Maybe the bakers made a mistake.

"I know what these are," Ryan said. He took my Oreo from Maria's hand and sniffed it as if the scent had all the answers. "They're oreos."

"Shut up, Ryan," Carlos spat.

What?

"They're oreos. Not with a capital O. Just oreos," Ryan explained. "Brand oreos."

Brand oreos. Was that what food was called when it didn't have the popular brand name? Brand-this, brand-that? It made no sense, but Ryan sounded like he knew what he was talking about.

So they're still Oreos.

"No, Ronnie, they're not Oreos. They're just oreos."

I ate my oreo and then Maria's Oreo. Hers tasted better. Sweeter. I looked at my bag of cookies.

Just oreos. Just brand oreos. I felt lonely within our lonely group.

Soon after the oreos incident, school was closed for holiday. Until after New Year's. On the last bus ride of the year, my bus driver gave us all candy canes and wished us a merry Christmas. The days leading up to Christmas weren't too interesting. Christmas was never a big deal for me. I liked the idea of gift-giving and being grateful for the miracle of Jesus, I really did. I liked the weird music with the funny cartoony voices. We listened to it in the van. I especially liked spending my afternoons home watching Christmas specials with Brendan. The animation made me laugh even when there wasn't anything funny happening. I just wanted to play with the characters – they all looked like toys. I'd wrap my Barbie blanket around my shoulders and keep Brendan in my lap and we'd remain in front of the television for who knows how long.

Mum didn't mind. Back home, she used to always encourage me to go outside, but here, after she fell on the sidewalk while taking out the trash, she stressed for me to stay inside. The poor woman's skin was even breaking out into little red bumps that turned into cold sores thanks to the weather (according to her). I was fine with it – the fact that I could stay inside, not the cold sores. Heat and television was much more welcoming. Brendan agreed with me.

We always hated the idea of cutting down a tree and plopping it in our house just for one day of the year, all to toss it out later. So, instead of going out and buying a Christmas tree (which we couldn't afford anyways), Dad bought a leafy plant about my height. The stem wasn't strong enough to hold any ornaments, so we placed the five-pack of plastic round red ornaments on the soil instead. A leafy plant growing out of Christmas-ornament soil. Mum loved it; we all did. In fact, it was loved so much that Dad said he was inviting some people over for a surprise. I knew it would be Uncle Larry, and maybe some of Uncle Larry's family since Dad had used "some people" instead of "someone."

To prepare for Christmas day, I dusted the furniture and tidied my room. The perk about not having much things was that cleaning was a breeze. Mum neatly placed a few wrapped packages by the Christmas plant.

And Dad bought a pack of just oreos.

Dad?

"Yes, Ronnie?"

Next time, could you buy Oreos?

"That's what these are. You can't see?"

No, those are oreos. Just oreos.

"Or maybe you're just losing your mind." Dad placed the oreos on the dining table. "Oreos are Oreos."

Poor Dad didn't know. I thought it'd be safe to just let him think the way he did so he wouldn't feel bad.

On Christmas, my family and I gathered on the floor in the living room and read some verses from the Bible. We took turns praying. Dad went first. His was brief and to the point, like his writing. Mum's was long, but fun to listen to. Every now and then she dropped a little joke with God and we'd all chuckle and God would chuckle a bit too. Then when it was my turn, I cleared my throat and thanked God for Jesus and Christmas specials. Afterwards, Mum spent the rest of the afternoon cooking in the kitchen while I was in charge of bathing and clothing Brendan.

Then our guest(s) arrived. First it was Uncle Larry. No one was behind him, so when I let him in, I was surprised to shut the door without someone's hand stopping the swing. As expected, Uncle Larry wore a bright red sweater with ugly embroidery somewhat resembling a reindeer. It looked like something a blind great-aunt would knit.

Where's the others?

"This is it, Ronnie Nose." Uncle Larry gestured at himself. "Disappointed?"

I thought your family was coming.

"You got ticket money for that? Because I don't." He laughed and roughed up my hair, which was plaited into two long braids.

Now Uncle Larry did not come empty-handed. He brought sorrel and two presents, along with a Santa hat that he pulled out from his back pocket and stuffed over my head. Uncle Larry was fun. You didn't need anyone else to make you smile if you had an Uncle Larry around. He always brought a gift and always brought the entertainment. This time, the entertainment was both himself and a boom box. He had to leave to get it from his car, and when he brought the big silver machine in, I dove for it. There were so many clickable buttons, and two big speakers on each side. Dad made me back off while Larry tucked in a tape and pressed the play button with a satisfying click. There was the softest whissing noise.

A deep voice rang out from the dark speakers. "Dashing through the snow..."

I sang with the man in the boom box. I danced around with Brendan until I got "too wild" and was told to put him down. Uncle Larry danced a goofy two-step.

"Wind your hips, saga boy," Dad said as he bopped up and down with a relaxed Brendan in his arms.

Uncle Larry laughed and wagged his finger at Dad. "Got to behave on Christmas, man."

And that was when our second guest arrived at the door. We were busy, so Mum stalked through the living room while wiping her hands with a dish rag.

Suddenly, I wished the man in the boom box would stop singing. I wished that Dad would stop bopping and that Uncle Larry would stop his two-step. I wished we had an actual Christmas tree in the corner. I wished we had more than just oreos for desert.

"Ms. Hurt, come on in, sweetie. I just finished cooking," Mum greeted.

The music didn't lower, not even a little, and Dad and Uncle Larry didn't stop moving. Brendan even spit up on Dad's shirt, just to make this more embarrassing.

Ms. Hurt stepped inside like she was testing a pool for warmth. She crept softly on the carpet and nodded her head when Dad and Uncle Larry offered her a wave. When she reached the dining room table, she finally stripped off her big coat – the same tall one she wore to walk home from work. She looked like an angel. Draped over her body was a white knit sweater dress and rosewood stockings. When her hood was removed, my eyes were glued to her hair. It was straight. Straight, and really long. And shiny. I imagined a halo over her head as we all joined her and Mum around the table.

Uncle Larry blessed the food and we all ate Mum's Christmas ham and macaroni pie and bread. We drank the sorrel Uncle Larry brought, but Mum poured water in my glass to make it less concentrated. Brendan was perfectly pleased slapping a spoon with his moist baby hands. We didn't say much while we ate. Mum said that meant the food was real good – which it was, but that wasn't why I was quiet. I was quiet because I was afraid. Ms. Hurt ate everything Mum prepared. She ate slow and noiseless, almost to the point where you couldn't tell she was chewing at all. She pretended to not notice the crack in my plate or the plant surrounded by ornaments in the corner. I continued to stare at her hair. Her tamed hair.

After supper we moved to the living room to exchange gifts. Uncle Larry got a bottle opener that came attached to a key chain. Mum got a gold necklace with a heart pendant from Dad. Dad got a new pair of khakis and a plain navy blue wristwatch from Mum. Brendan got a teething ring from my parents and a little knit hat from Uncle Larry. I received three gifts, one from my parents, one from my uncle, and one from Ms. Hurt. A new shirt. A hat that matched Brendan's. And a football.

A round ball with little strips of blue. From Ms. Hurt.

And Ms. Hurt got a pair of glittery studs. Her face lit up like a Christmas plant and she held each individual earring in front of her earlobes. She stared directly at me and I instinctively nodded in approval. She put them down and smiled her Hurt smile. The smile that threatened to be a complete smile, but one corner of her lips never quirked up enough to be symmetric with the other. Her smile reminded me of the sidewalks back home.

"It's beautiful. Thank you," she said. Her voice still sounded dry, but full. "I love studs," she added, not speaking to anyone in particular.

Mum left to go handle the dirty dining table after that, and Dad and Uncle Larry followed her to help out. Ms. Hurt offered her help, but they said no, she was the guest. Uncle Larry was over so often he wasn't even considered a guest anymore.

So it was just me and a woman with tamed red hair and glittery studs left in the living room, sitting on opposite couches. I felt ashamed that our couch colors clashed and didn't even remotely look like they came from the same set. I wished we had a tree. I wished "Frosty the Snowman" wasn't playing while we stared at each other.

I thought Mum had come to the rescue when she walked in the living room again, but all she did was tell us to help ourselves to oreos while she put Brendan down for his nap. The boring white package of manhole cookies were dropped on the coffee table. The plastic read *Sandwich Cookies*. Not oreos. Not any other fun name. Just a name that stated exactly what it was.

Strangely enough, Ms. Hurt didn't waste any time. She leaned forward and tore the plastic, revealing the tray of black and white. Her face expressionless, she took an oreo out. Then she took another. And another. Three oreos stacked on her palm.

"I love these," she told me, looking almost embarrassed about her childish stacking game. She held her hand out towards me and I took an oreo from the top.

I watched her teeth crunch into the cookie, some strands of her hair getting in her mouth. It made me happy. She didn't quite tame it all the way.

They're not Oreos, you know.

Clawing the stray hairs off her cheeks, she looked at me funny. "I know. They're brand, but what's the difference? I have the same ones at home."

And that was enough encouragement for me. I reached for another cookie.

Later on, Mum and Dad and Uncle Larry joined us in the living room and we drank more sorrel and ate more oreos. We were listening to "Do You Hear What I Hear?" when the topic of family was brought up again. Uncle Larry thanked Ms. Hurt for "sacrificing" her time to join us for Christmas. Ms. Hurt stated with her familiar hollowness that she wasn't sacrificing anything.

"I've got no other family to go to, it was no big deal," she had said.

Are they on another island?

Ms. Hurt looked from Uncle Larry to me.

"Everywhere is an island," Uncle Larry explained.

Ms. Hurt bit her lip as if she were considering this idea. Then she picked up her glittery studs from the coffee table and studied them. "Imagine stripping the earth of all its water. All the oceans, just gone. It'll just be one big round crumb of land. The earth is an island itself."

Uncle Larry had already turned back to Mum and Dad, cracking a joke with them, probably. No one was listening. My attention never swayed.

So we're all stuck.

Ms. Hurt's brown eyes looked up from the earrings. "If you look at it that way." She picked up another *Sandwich Cookie* and twisted it so that it would separate without breaking the icing. Then she slapped them back together again. Raking her free hand through her dead hair, she shrugged.

I like your hair better wild, Jessica.

I helped myself to another cookie as well. From the way I saw it now, we were both OK with being stuck together, even if we were just brand oreos.

This Big Isle

Because it was so cold outside and winter wouldn't be over for another couple months, I didn't really get to know any of the kids in the neighborhood. I couldn't see them unless they were on my bus. I did get to familiarize myself with the people living in the apartment building, though. There were two families living on the very bottom floor. One family consisted of Africans. On Sunday mornings I'd occasionally catch them walking up the stairs in their Sunday clothes, which really looked like big thick sheets of fabric questionably secured around their bodies and heads. The other family was a group of blond-haired, blue-eyed dolls who looked like the Barbie on my bed sheet. The second floor was a very loud floor. Directly below our apartment, a clan of Hispanic men in blue jumpsuits played flashy music and watched television shows with actors that spoke so fast I never caught what the lines were (unless, looking back at it now, perhaps they were speaking Spanish). Next to them lived an old, dusty woman and her grandson who seemed to be taking care of her. I felt sorry for her because of all the get-togethers her neighbors tended to throw, but then her grandson mentioned to me that she was "basically deaf" and could "sleep through a fire drill."

Then there was *my* neighbor. A dark skinny man with dreadlocks and black eyes. Dad called him "Mop Man," because every time we passed him in the hallway Dad gets tempted to flip him upside and clean the floor with his hair. Mop Man didn't seem to like me, or anybody for that matter. I tried to say hi to him a couple of times, but he typically ignored me and flew a little faster up the stairs. His mind always seemed to be racing. I gave up after a while, but then things changed one morning. For no particular reason, I woke up from a blank-dream and couldn't fall back asleep, so I found just lying in bed and staring at the ceiling, five in the morning. I crept through the living room so I could get a glass of tap water, but I heard a light tap dance sound from outside the front door, like knives scraping on the floor. I wasn't tall enough to peek through the peephole, so I waited for the knives to hush before unlocking the door and opening it just a crack.

I was staring at a Pit bull. Actually, I was staring at two Pit bulls. They were muscular like miniature bodybuilding horses, and their heads were as heavy and wide as their necks. The worst part of this encounter was that the Pits were both staring back. I wanted to gulp the way Jerry did when Tom had him trapped, but I didn't. I was smarter than that. I shut the door quietly. *Click.* All I knew was that Mop Man had two horses on a leash, and I caught him. After that, any time we came across one another, he'd smile and wave and pretend like I made his day. He pretended that I made his day because all I had to do was tell my parents to open the door at five in the morning, and by doing that, I would ruin his year. Turns out, pets weren't allowed in Scapeview Apartments. Mop Man didn't like me, but I have to admit, I enjoyed how much he feared me. I felt in control for once.

And speaking of control, I tried to make sure for the New Year that I'd do better in school. Not academically. Socially. I asked my Dad for a little journal and he bought me it the same day. He got all bright and happy, thinking I'd fill the pages with beautiful metaphors and works of fiction like he used to back when he had the time to be happy. Unfortunately, I was a reader, not a writer, and I knew that wouldn't change.

I filled the journal with a bunch of personal notes. A lengthy bulleted list of guidelines that should have made my interactions with other people "less foreign." People didn't say "rubbish" here, they just said *trash*. "Chips" were just *fries*, or *French fries*. "Woogies" were *hair-ties*, or *ponytail-holders*, or *scrunchies*. Scrunchie was my favorite because it was almost as fun to say as woogie. "Standard five" was *grade five*. Measurements used *feet* and *inches*, not "meters." I also wrote down little pronunciations tips and reminders as well. Usually when I said something wrong, someone would repeat it at school. Now we were well into the winter holiday (oh, they don't say "holiday," they say *break* or *vacation*) and I got my journal the day after Christmas. I found it pretty easy to remember all the mistakes I made at school. My classmates didn't allow me to forget, and neither would my journal.

Never ever say "chuh-pid" – it's "STOO-pid"

Never ever say "tree" – it's "THUH-ree"

Never ever say "yuh" – it's "U"

Never ever ignore the G at the end of words – runninG, cryinG

Never ever ignore the R at the end of words – ponytail-holdeR,

Never every say "Mum" – it's Mom

I crossed the last one off because to me, Mum wasn't a word, it was a name.

I titled my journal "tips for an oreo." When I proudly showed Dad on New Year's Eve, his face fell. He skimmed through the thirty pages I scribbled in, pausing to read a few lines and skipping the next. Then he closed the book and held it out to me as far away from his body as possible.

"You didn't capitalize the 'o' in Oreo."

Before I could explain that the type of oreo I was referring to was a different kind, Dad went into his room and shut the door. To me, he had to be mad at either two things: my capitalization mistake, or the "papers." The "papers" hadn't been brought up since we moved to the apartment, but I know its spirit lived in all of us.

So on this New Year's Eve, the spirit of the Papers haunted the apartment. There was leftover snow from the days that passed, and it wasn't as cold as it was on Christmas. Mum let me go outside and play in the snow.

Okay, I'm not going outside to play. I just need to cool down.

Mum thought this was the funniest thing in the world and said she had to tell Dad that his daughter mastered the pun. Dad said that it wasn't even a pun.

"Your sense of humor is so weird. Are you pregnant again?" Dad asked.

It was all a bunch of nonsense to me so I left without saying anything. Embraced by my big marshmallow coat and squeaking boots, I trudged through the frozen layers of cotton. I wanted to pick up a clump of snow and find a snowflake that looked like the ones my class cut out during art the week before holiday. Not wanting to lose feeling in my fingers, I searched my coat for my climbing gloves. I tugged the left one on, but when I stuck my hand in for the next glove, all I felt was the plush interior of my pocket. No red and black glove to match the first.

I spotted a forest green car approaching the building, and I wasn't in the mood to talk to anyone. The snow didn't do anything but penetrate my socks. I darted into the building, flying up the stairs and speeding through the apartment with a trail of flames as the only trace of me. I don't remember what I was thinking at the time because I wasn't thinking at all. I stripped off my winter clothes. My gloved hand slammed the bathroom door while my naked hand slid open the bathroom mirror. On the top shelf of the hidden cabinet where a few shards of glass. I grabbed one, just one, by locking my knees onto the surface of the sink. Then I hopped off and closed the cabinet so I could stare at myself in the mirror the same way Dad did in the Hurt basement. I couldn't get my face to wrinkle enough for parallel lines on my forehead, but letting my eyes drip tears was easy. I flung off my left glove so I could hold the glass up to my wrist.

I know. It was a stupid idea. I was stupid for thinking this would solve anything. At the time, though, I didn't know. All I knew was that my Dad was the smartest man alive and chose to slide glass across his skin when he felt just awful. The fact that he kept a few pieces in our new bathroom meant to me that the habit was worth the trouble. People ask me all the time why I was "sick" enough to resort to self-harm.

I wasn't sick. I was worried.

Worried about what? I was just a kid. That was it. The best part about being ten was the fact that the only thing I had to worry about was my parents. And honestly, that was the worst part, too.

I don't know what I was expecting to happen when I cut my wrist. I was in utter shock when I felt my warm blood leak through the little gash I made. It hurt. Maybe more than your average cut because I was staring at it and thinking of nothing else. Or maybe it was because the only thing truly hurting me at that very moment was me.

The door swung open and Dad flew in before I could do more damage – not that I minded. I was grateful, even, and terrified to do it again.

"I knew you knew," Dad said the words as if each one was a needle to his tongue.

I said nothing as he took the piece of glass from me. He took the other ones from the shelf. He then stood over the bathroom rubbish and individually dropped each piece of glass into the basket.

"I did that nonsense because all I was giving you and your mother was OK, not the best." He washed my cut and stuck a bandage over it. Then, he lifted me to his side, carrying me through the bathroom doorway.

I hadn't been picked up since I was six. I kicked too much, didn't want to be tamed by anyone's grasp. Somehow this time my feet dangled lifelessly.

"But then your mother told me that *my* best was *the* best."

Mum is smart.

Dad laughed. "You think I'd marry just anyone?"

So Dad didn't advise me not to cut myself, not that I needed the advice by that point. Instead, he left the conversation at that. Like he knew I wasn't planning on doing this ever again. I just wanted to try it. Study it. I was his "child genius" after all.

We reached the living room. There were two of my favorite people in the planet: a man wearing bright clothes that clashed with his dark skin, and a woman with hair like a desert fire. Dad set me down and bent over to slip on his black socks, exposing his soft, pale feet. This was a good sign, a very good sign.

Uncle Larry whipped out his New Year's Eve survival kit, which was just a single paper party hat and a sack of kurma. Mum tried to fixate the cone on Brendan's head, but he whined and wiggled so much we felt sorry for him and removed it. So I had the honor.

We ate the finger-shaped fried dough and drank sorrel (mine, as usual, was watered down) and laughed and danced along to Uncle Larry's tapes. Ms. Hurt remained timid, not talking a whole lot, but when she did, her voice was full. Not hollow like it used to be. She even held Brendan for the first time and snuck him a brief kiss on the cheek. I took the opportunity to show her my journal.

"Tips for an oreo," she read. She looked at me. "Nice."

I watched her as she skimmed through the pages, fumbling a bit because she only had one free hand. She smirked at certain lines, but at one point, her lips formed a straight line.

What?

"But I like that you sound like you're singing." She held out the journal page towards me.

To avoid "don't you have the cutest accent?" from a shoe store clerk, never ever sing when you speak.

I frowned.

And I like that your hair looks like fire.

"Let's make a deal, then."

I leaned closer.

"I won't straighten my hair if you never stop singing."

Okay.

I took the journal back from her and we shook hands. I promised I'd never stop singing. And we laughed. But I couldn't steer away from our conversation just yet.

Can I touch your hair?

Ms. Hurt jumped to get Brendan a little further up her hip. "Sure, but your finger might get stuck," she said halfheartedly.

I smiled. I let my hand graze against her hair. It felt worn out. Dense. Warm. Busy as if it were a reflection of her mind. My fingers were snakes in a tumbleweed. I never felt hair like that before. Absolutely wild, just like me. Wild, but stuck to her head.

Stuck to a crumb.

Later that night, we all gathered by the window in our dining room, the same window that showed us our first sight of snow. Dad gave us some instructions. I looked back to check the clock in the living room. It only read seven o'clock. But then Dad pulled open the window, letting an icy gust of God's breath into the apartment. It was dark outside; the street lights making the dirty snow on the ground seem to sparkle. Brendan and I were wearing our matching knit hats.

All six of us stuck our heads out the window and screamed to Scapeview Apartments and Spring Homes and Scottsville, Pennsylvania, America.

Happy New Year!

And when the moment was over, we huddled back inside to cower from the cold.

Why did we do that?

"It was Larry and I's idea," Dad said proudly.

"I wanted to say it while we were all still awake," Uncle Larry added.

Ms. Hurt helped Mum shut the window. "It's the New Year somewhere."

She was right. On this island, the year had already begun. Tamika and Marissa were probably with each other, having a party in one of their houses. Adam was with them. Mr. Jimmy's garden store was closed and he was probably sitting on his deck in a sticky porch chair with sleeping grandkids on his lap. Uncle Jimmy and Auntie Jemma were probably at a club in another state, dancing and waiting for midnight to kiss. Lenny was under the earth, screaming Happy New Year because he didn't know any better.

I pictured Grandma outside the step-house, lying above Lenny on the grass by Butch's chains. Her spiny fingers were clenching the silver links tightly because as much as Butch loved her and she loved him, she knew he was a wild thing and had to be held. I pictured her with no one else. No man friend. Just Butch and Lenny and maybe a mango in her hand.

Dad interrupted my thoughts by pushing my journal into my stomach.

"Listen to me very carefully," he began. "Add this to the end of your *tips*."

144

I held the book.

"Throw this journal away, and never, ever read it again."

Dad was the smartest man I knew, so I disappeared into the bathroom and dropped the journal into the rubbish with the ripped toothpaste box and broken glass.

At eight o'clock I stepped away from my family for a moment to open the window again and stare out at the white-covered road, yelling Happy New Year again for every stuck person out there.

The streets here weren't really gold, or even remotely close. In fact, it was just asphalt: the same exact material used to pave the roads where I came from. Nothing new. Nothing interesting. Gold streets are in heaven and nowhere else. But I didn't care. I didn't care at all. I still don't care. On this big crumb of an island, our home is where the asphalt is.

And that's OK with me.

Epilogue

Dear Grandma,

I received a prompt in English class that says to write to someone from your childhood that you miss. I wrote to Adam, Tamika's older brother, and my teacher gave me an A. Then she said, "You know what'd be a cool prompt? If the assignment was to write to someone you *don't* miss." We laughed. Well, *they* laughed. I didn't; I was thinking of you

Don't get me wrong – I'll never forget you, or Butch, who was practically an extension of you. I'll never forget how you ate my mangoes and refused to share food and killed my goat and buried him underneath you. I'll never forget how you told us to go. Honestly, that was the wisest thing you've ever said. *Go.* We all knew you weren't going to change, even you knew – so why didn't we just leave? Why didn't we just *go*?

I've had and still have a ton of questions that I can't answer alone. Why don't we ever speak to Uncle Johnny anymore? Why is our mail still under Uncle Larry's name? Why did I miss school on Tuesday to answer mostly drug-related questions from a middle-aged, bald stranger in a blue uniform? Why do my parents refuse to let me apply for a job? What are "the papers?"

I'm not stupid, and my ability to eavesdrop has improved greatly since you last saw me. I've learned what "the papers" mean to us, but I've never been clued in on what they actually are. I just know that somewhere on the top left corner of one of them, my name and birth date are written in bold. There is one thing I've learned, though. G.W. means Good Will. Mum and Dad still refer to the thrift store that way, even though I'm sure they know that I've figured it out.

You probably don't care but Dad picked up a pen last week, and it wasn't to sign his name on a check. It was to write. He wrote. I can't even remember the last time he sat down to write things, beautiful things. Whatever it was, it had stanzas and his attempt at cursive writing. The other day he told me something I won't ever forget. *People are like books, because books are never really finished.* He was a little drunk that night, but he made me think. Are we ever really finished? Does anyone ever die truly satisfied with what they've done in life? Might as well try to get to that point, right?

So I think things are going well. I mean, Mum is the secretary for this old woman who adores her accent probably more than her work ethic, and Brendan is the best reader in his first grade class. I play soccer.

I'm kidding. I play football.

Uncle Larry is still kicking. Turns out he's much older than I had thought. He hid his age well with his clothes. Now he's got a lung disease but we visit whenever we can, and we're going to keep visiting until he can call me Ronnie Nose without coughing. When I sit beside his bed with my history homework he likes to make stuff up about America. He said there's going to be a Black president before he dies. I told him he had to live another hundred years before that would ever happen.

Ms. Hurt is doing well, too. You wouldn't know her, thank God, but I think if you did, you wouldn't dislike her all that much. She's like a younger version of you: funny, honest. Real blunt. The big difference is she has this stunning, wild set of red hair. Plus she's a wonderful human being to be around.

There are so many things I could tell you right now. I've made new friends. They love braiding my hair after practice, and while my parents still refuse to let me come over their houses, I'm pretty sure one day they will. Surprisingly enough, I also have a crush on this boy at school. He's no athlete when it comes to sports, but the kid can run. And climb. Usually I speak American when I'm outside the apartment, but I've become so comfortable with this guy that my accent slips from time to time. He actually thinks it's cute. Says I shouldn't hide it anymore. One day I won't have to. Dad's working on it.

You know, I love you very much. I care about your health and your loneliness and your relationship with that friend of yours. Maybe you have a TV now – if so, good for you. I hope Butch is still alive to keep you company. If he's not, you should bury him next to Lenny. They could be friends.

Dad mailed you our phone number a few months after moving into the apartment (that was five years ago, Grandma) in case you wanted to check up on us. See if we're OK. We hope that you are. Dad was going to resend the number again, but he decided there was just no point. So, we do love you, we just don't like you very much, Grandma. The feeling is most likely mutual. That's why, out of the unconditional respect I have left for you, I'd never, ever send you this letter.

Take care.

From the streets of ~~gold~~ melted gold,

Ronnelle Khan

Ronnelle Khan
The Granddaughter Who Moved On

About the Author

Brittany Maylyn Du Bois was born on the small island of Trinidad & Tobago. After moving to the United States, her interest in writing began the moment she was able to press pen to paper. She grew up with discrimination and identity-confusion, as being a mixed child of interracial parents and an immigrant in the early 21st century was still a curious matter. Former Literary Arts student of the magnet high school, Carver Center for Arts and Technology, she fully recognizes that the best way to share true human experience is to have someone experience it with her and through her. This is her first novel.

Made in the USA
Middletown, DE
23 May 2016